I0451091

LAST
BLAST

GLENN A. BRUCE

This is a work of fiction. Names, characters, places, and incidents are products of the author's imagination or are used fictitiously and are not to be construed as real. Any resemblance to actual events, locations, organizations, or persons, living or dead, is entirely coincidental.

World Castle Publishing, LLC
Pensacola, Florida
Copyright © Glenn A. Bruce 2020
Paperback ISBN: 9781953271624
eBook ISBN: 9781953271631
First Edition World Castle Publishing, LLC, February 15, 2021
http://www.worldcastlepublishing.com
Licensing Notes
Cover: Karen Fuller
Editor: Maxine Bringenberg

CHAPTER ONE

In Atlanta, a few minutes before the midday news update at CNN, two anchors sat in their chairs getting last-minute touch-ups by the makeup department. They had both been rushed upstairs to deliver what would become "the biggest story of this century."

The female anchor, a pretty Asian-American woman, named Meghan Carter, had just turned forty-two but looked ten years younger. She sat frozen, staring ahead, while one of CNN's premier hair-and-makeup artists finished the sharp line on her mascara. Sitting next to her, getting similar eye treatment over his darker base, sat Jim Malloy, fifty-three, African American, also a decade younger in appearance.

Without moving, more because she was petrified about delivering this story than making sure her makeup did not get smeared, Meghan asked Jim, "Are you ready for this?"

He said clearly, "No."

Seven hundred miles to the north, in the otherwise calm neighborhood of South Akron, Ohio, just below Akron proper, a line of ATF cars, vans, and trucks lined a tranquil street as a CNN field vehicle whipped up and parked, already raising its antenna. A reporter and her cameraman leapt out and hurried for the cops, doing camera and voice checks as they went.

In the studio, a voice came over the loudspeakers from the booth. "All right, people. We're on in ten…nine.…"

The makeup folks did final cursory checks of their anchors' faces then cleared the set. Cameras locked in place. Not a word was said in the studio, though in the booth, controlled chaos ruled "the roost," as the news team called it.

"How's my remote?"

"Sinclair and Hastings are both in place and ready."

"Signal is up."

"And…cue the stage."

A producer off camera said, "We're on in five…four.…"

Meghan Carter and Jim Malloy tensed up more than they had been seconds earlier. Each took a steadying breath as the count got to "two," and the floor director pointed at them.

Meghan counted to one in her head and said, "Good noon, America. Well, it has happened. Outgoing President Nestor E. Navarro signed legislation sent to him by the 115th Congress before their final recess."

Jim took over: "The eleventh-hour bill passed both houses before ten o'clock this morning and was on the president's desk by ten-fifty. He signed at precisely eleven-fifteen, just forty-five minutes ago—"

Meghan could not wait her turn. She said, "Outlawing—" as Jim said, "Outlawing all—"

Both paused to look at each other, tense and apologetic, and said, together again, as one, "I'm sorry."

Jim said, "Go ahead, Meghan. Please."

Meghan said, "Yes, Jim. Thanks. It is exciting and dangerous news."

They shared another nervous glance, flashing uncertain smiles as.…

***

Somewhere in central Ohio, a family of five sat clustered on their sofa. The paternal head of the family urged Meghan to, "Say it."

Angelo Miller was solidly middle-American—white, fifty-nine, and chronically unemployed. Six years without a real job. A third-generation factory man, he loved his Hamm's beer and red meat and went by Big Angie because he was large and hated being called Angelo. Lots of other guys kidded him, calling him Angela, which had led to more than one altercation.

After the auto parts plant closed, laying him off with 672 other skilled UAW workers when it moved to Mexico, Big Angie become bitter. After three weeks as a "sweeper" at Burger King—he had no idea how to work a register or take orders from drive-up—he quit in disgrace. A series of other small and meaningless jobs served only to humiliate the once-proud union man and throw him into a deep funk that only got worse with time, his sense of self and self-worth unravelling faster than his old cotton robe.

When his unemployment insurance ran out, Angie was forced to admit he was free-falling. His kids were grown— Eric, thirty-two, married to Allison, thirty-two, with two kids; and daughter Erica, thirty, married to a terminal loser everyone called Ferdie, twenty-eight, a bastardization of his name Fred/Freddie, with three kids—so Angie afforded himself "forced early retirement," as he preferred to call it.

Two years before, Big Anj had given up trying to find work and settled into his La-Z-Boy for the duration. He found FoxNews and never left—all day, every day, every show. His world view changed, becoming "limited," as his wife Twyla told her few friends patiently. Twyla had hoped Angie would "snap out of it" at some point and find work. Instead, he gave up.

And got angry.

His rage grew over the years to the point that even a commercial for a real estate company would set him off. "Goddamn fuckin' real-a-tors! Who do they think can buy a fuckin' house in this market? Goddamn spic president."

In truth, the market was the best it had been in a decade. But on Fox, not so much. They had been too busy hating on President Nestor Navarro to bother with any facts that might make him look not so awful.

Twyla had been given her name because her mother hoped she would be a dancer, and, as a small child, Twyla did dance. She was not the star of her class, but she loved it. Little Twyla-Anne felt a freedom in dance class as nowhere else. By the time she made it to high school, her parents had divorced, her mother had died, her father had married a semi-illiterate whore from his favorite bar, and Twyla was left to fend for herself. No more dancing — except for that month in Exquisite Kittens. But one forced blowjob from the owner, and she quit. On to greater things near the end of the car parts line as a trainee in quality control.

A few years later, Twyla met Angelo "Big Angie" Miller outside the factory. He worked in assembly. They hit it off. Twyla would later get promoted, but giving birth to Eric, then Erica less than two years later, put her back at home, mothering. All that was fine until the kids were grown and Twyla got itchy to do something again. Big Angie, being "traditional," as he liked to say of his 1950s misogynistic tendencies, was against it. But Twyla's "whining" finally got to him, and he relented. She was forty-eight at the time.

Her first excursion back into the workforce was as a

sweeper at the same Burger King, from which Angie would later take "early retirement" after three weeks of contentious employment—mainly endlessly grousing about the "punk" high school kids who *did* know how to work a register and take orders at the drive-thru. A decade before, Twyla had done better. She learned to work the headset, trained on the register and, in a corporate push to promote women, quickly became an assistant manager.

When her pay did not increase to suit Angie's demands, Twyla looked elsewhere and found a better job at a Cracker Barrel. The commute was longer—twenty-six miles each way—but she enjoyed the job and alone-time in the car. Her coworkers were "more like me," she said—her age and background—and despite the fast, demanding work, they all got along.

Twyla thrived away from home.

Then Angie got laid off, could not find real work, and descended into the work-free hell of too much time to criticize the world while picking up a new hobby: gun ownership. Angie Miller had always liked guns, but now, thanks to FoxNews and endless NRA commercials, he *needed* them—for "personal protection." He clarified, "From the blacks." It claimed his "goddamned Second Amendment right, goddammit," and he planned to exercise it—repeatedly.

To Twyla's memory, Angie had never been overtly racist. The factory had a diverse workforce, and Big Anj was known for his ability to get along with everyone—even if he couldn't take a joke about his name. Otherwise, he was a "go along to get along" kind of guy. He would tell you that himself—sometimes twice in one day. But all of that changed when Big Anj found O'Reilly and O'Hannity and those two former New York judges who seemed less impartial judicial experts than kangaroo court jesters. He started blaming "the blacks" for everything that was wrong with America, like Archie Bunker reborn. "Them and the spics." And the "damned Muslims," of course. He only bitched about the "chinks" when the price of electronics went up on rare occasions.

Ramen.

Twyla held her tongue. Her favorite coworker was a black woman named Sheila, from twenty-six miles in the other direction. They were a great team, both assistant managers with overlapping shifts at lunch, their busiest time next to the interstate. The work proved hard and fast, but steady — and rewarding. Customer compliments ran high.

Twyla was happy for the first time in close to two decades.

Then Angie started complaining about her hours. Twyla did not get home until nine most nights — or a little later, depending on the dinner rush — by which time Angie lazed, well-sauced.

"Where's my beer?" was about the only greeting he ever gave his wife anymore. Twyla's "one job," as Angie saw it, was stopping for his twelve-pack of Miller Lite on her way home every night. She paid for it out of her tips so it would not show up on their credit card. Twyla was afraid the government might check on them at some point, and the IRS might see that Angie spent a lot of money on beer instead of looking for work. Unemployment might show up asking for their money back — ideas put in her head by Angie, who had come to distrust the government.

Distrust that morphed into abhorrence.

At first, Big Angie Miller hated all government; then, he got more selective. "Goddamn fuckin' liberals ruining this goddamn country right and left. Every goddamn time you turn around, they're givin' more of our hard-earned tax money away to more no-good, worthless, lazy, shiftless…"

Fill in the blank.

Sitting in his La-Z-Boy drinking beer paid for by his wife's tips, Angie was mad as hell, and he wasn't going to take it anymore—whatever it was. And he had never even seen that movie. He didn't like movies, just wrestling and Fox—and occasionally CNN to see what "the enemy" was up to.

"Say it, goddamn it, you Chinese fucking cunt!" he shouted from his La-Z-Boy at the television, choosing CNN to harangue over breaking the bad news.

Twyla said, "Angie. The kids."

Their grandchildren sat wide-eyed, staring at their fat, angry grandpa, then looking quizzically at their parents for answers.

Eric said, "It's all right, Mom. They've heard it before. They gotta grow up sometime. This crap with the government has to stop somewhere."

"Yeah, well, this is it, right here," his father said.

Erica took a more palliative approach. "Dad," she said. "It's just…kinda watch the cussing in front of the kids, okay? Please?"

Since she was a daddy's girl, Angie grunted something like approval as one of the grandkids—he didn't care which one—said, "Can we watch something else?" and one of the parents—Angie didn't listen to which one—said, "No dear. This is important. It's history."

That much was true. The Millers had not paid attention to history in 2017 and nearly lost the house. This time, the entire extended family had been sitting in front of the television for two hours, waiting for history to happen.

To Big Angie, two hours represented nothing. He had been waiting six years for this moment—in his head, his "whole damn life" — thereby rewriting his own history. But who was counting? If anyone in the Miller clan was, they were not saying.

Wise caution or cautious wisdom — either worked with *Dad*.

Twyla watched her husband and wrung a towel in her hands, deeply concerned over what was about to happen in the nation and her home. She still had her job at Cracker Barrel and did not want to lose it to "those damn crazies," as even she called them.

Whoever they were.

At CNN, Meghan and Jim finished their awkward niceties and prepared to move on with the big news. Meghan said, "It's a big story, Jim. The biggest this reporter has ever brought to the American people."

Jim said, "I understand." His smile was genuine. He had broken big stories before. He was older. This was *her* moment.

Angie could not wait. "Say it, goddammit!" he dared the TV lady, challenging her to spill on what he already knew she was going to say.

The grandkids twisted on the floor, bored, and Twyla twisted her towel, mortified, as on the small flat-screen television, Meghan Carter said, "Guns, all guns...guns in America...all of America..."

Angie rocked his La-Z-Boy up and shouted at the television, "Goddammit, SAY it, you fucking cunt! Say it, or I will personally come down there and make you say it, China Girl!"

Twyla pled, "Anj, please. Calm down."

"Calm down? Why?!" Angie shouted at her. He knew what Meghan Carter was about to say. He could feel it coming — the loss of his personal religious freedom.

Erica said, "You'll bust a vein, Daddy," and the kids laughed.

Big Angie ignored them all and, for the last time, ordered Meghan to, "Saaaaay it." He wanted closure—and purpose.

Meghan said it. "…Illegal."

As the screen image went to the White House, Angie came out of his chair. "Goddamn spic, I knew it!"

He left the room.

At CNN, Jim Malloy said, "That's right. As of seventeen minutes ago, all guns are now illegal in the United States of America." He turned to his co-anchor. "I never thought I'd see this day, Meghan."

"Neither did I, Jim. It's a big day."

Angie screamed from another room, "Turn that damn thing off! Let's go! Move it!"

Dutifully, everyone jumped up, grandkids and all, and scurried to where Angie had slid open a "secret" panel at the end of the hall. Behind the false wall stood a steel door with two safe-style tumblers. Angie was already spinning the numbers.

He had it down. He had been practicing for a decade.

With the heavy door open, everyone poured inside and down the steps into the fortified basement, followed by Angie, who shut and locked the door on their prepper vault, which had a thousand gallons of water in hermetically sealed drums, a composting toilet, tight bunks like on a submarine, shelves full of food, hundreds of rolls of toilet paper, thousands of rounds of ammo. And guns—hundreds of guns.

Twyla was only now aware. So, that was where all the money had gone!

Eric had looked for the remote but couldn't find it, so no one had turned off the TV in the living room, which now held

on an exterior shot of the White House.
    Expectant.

CHAPTER TWO

Video of the People's House was old—stock footage of an average, calm day provided by the administration. Everyone for ten blocks around, including reporters—especially reporters—had been cleared out hours earlier. In truth, Pennsylvania Avenue lay surreally empty and quiet, not a tourist to be seen. But the number of armed troops made the White House look more like a tin-pot dictator's haunt—one expecting armed insurrection.

Not far off the mark.

Inside the Oval Office, chaos blended with panic. Everyone knew what was coming and what needed to be said to prepare the nation. The president's cabinet had been brought in for the announcement, as well as committee chairs from Congress—at least those who agreed with the new law. Everyone else had gone home to their respective states or were in hiding. One Senator took his entire family to Europe for a "long-planned extended vacation."

The president, Nestor E. Navarro—who went by Ed, shortened from his middle name of Eduardo—was getting his own last makeup touches in preparation for the historic address. Aides ran around like headless chickens, carrying glowing tablets and phones, sheaves of papers, overstuffed folders, and several versions of the words written by the president's speechwriters.

Other aides worked the shredders.

As black-ops looking Secret Service agents took posts every three feet around the roof of the White House, hundreds more combat-ready Marines took positions around the grounds, while five fully armored *loud* combat helicopters landed in the Rose Garden, surrounding Marine One, the president's ride.

Someone in the Oval Office freaked out. "Tell them to shut down! We're on in two minutes!"

Someone else ran outside and was immediately tackled by guards. The president watched, shaking his head, as the poor woman waved her hands excitedly and shouted complaints and orders, which were then transferred by a calmer Marine into his encrypted radio. The helicopters shut down.

A little over a minute later, a White House producer asked the president if he was ready, and he said, "Yes."

"Clear!" someone shouted, and everyone left the frame.

President "Ed" Navarro cleared his throat, reviewed his notes, then looked up into his teleprompter as an A.D. counted down: "Three...two...."

The president had thought about smiling as a signal of comfort but ultimately chose a look of somber reflection, consolidated power, acceptance of great change in the face of greater fixed resistance, and overall presidential confidence.

Steady at the helm.

"My fellow Americans," he said, as had every televised president before him. But there, custom and tradition ended. "Today, Congress passed, and I signed, a bill outlawing the ownership or possession of any and all guns in America. We will begin the collection of those now unlawful weapons immediately under the close scrutiny of the ATF and the FBI, as well as local and state police, to search for and seize all firearms of all types from all Americans. National Guard troops are also on the ground in key cities in the event of any large-scale disturbances, which are not anticipated."

Now, he smiled, both as a calmative and acknowledgment of a lie.

There was not a sound in the oval office — or anywhere else in America. Bars were packed.

Life stood still.

"I know this is controversial legislation with which many of you, my fellow Americans, do not agree. 'I feel your pain,' as another great Democrat once said. I *feel*...your pain."

A centrist Republican congressman rolled his eyes. Around the country, the silence ended. Moans and shouts were heard, and more than one TV set took the brunt of the country's displeasure with a shattering beer bottle.

President Ed went on. "This great country has always had a proud tradition of gun ownership, as mentioned in the Second Amendment to our glorious, old, and honored Constitution. However, the Second Amendment does not, *could* not have anticipated the types or volume of guns and the onerous uses to which these weapons would be put on a near daily basis some 260 years later. Last year alone, we had a new high of 62,453 deaths from guns in America. Injuries related to gun use added another 97,214 Americans to this awful SARS-6 pandemic."

President Navarro paused. Several advisers who knew the speech word for word drew a heavy breath. He then said, "Those numbers, those acts, are intolerable and can no longer be accepted. This is why I signed this legislation into law today."

The aide exhaled.

Navarro said, "My fellow Americans, we are no longer free. We have become slaves to our own dangerous self-interests. I contend that we are better than that, and we must take care of our own."

The president looked down at his notes, a way of adding a moment to build tension as much as to gather his courage for the punchline.

He looked up. "I foresee a coming age of peace and good fortune for our great nation, one in which every man, woman, and child may walk any street of any town, at any time of day or night, with no fear of assault from a deadly loaded weapon. That our children will once again feel safe in their schools, with no need for unsettling drills aimed at lessening the number of young deaths during a senseless, coldhearted attack. That our malls and churches will again be places for peaceful gathering and prayer, our parks and night clubs again free from the malignant threat of death for simply being in that place at that time."

Now came the clincher—the hardest part.

"To this end, I ask each and every one of you, my fellow Americans, to willingly and peacefully surrender your weapons when asked so that we may all walk together into this new era of peace and prosperity at home in this country we love, but that has sadly slipped off the rails of sanity."

His aides shuffled nervously, restless to leave the room and head to a nuclear bunker. Across America, drunks and half-drunks and cold-sober citizens were deciding whether they would comply with the president's request. The not-my-president types had already decided before they heard the speech that they would not give up without a fight. What that fight might look like was the question in their and everyone else's minds.

The president ended with, "Good afternoon and good luck."

CHAPTER THREE

In bars and grills across the land, a stampede for the doors was fully underway. Americans wanted to get home to their guns — or go hide from those folks who had guns. Having no idea how bad it might be, Congress called a recess.

Rumors abounded that some had applied for citizenship in Canada.

In Fishhook, Alaska, just north of Anchorage, with a population of just over five-thousand — forty-nine hundred of them gun owners — every officer and reserve officer had been called in and issued full riot gear. Nerves held taut. Everyone knew everyone else and generally did not fear each other. But with the president's announcement, fear was the predominant, if only, emotion in Fishhook.

In Delray Beach, Florida, retirees in a Golden Corral on US-1 stuffed even more dinner rolls and muffins into their purses and pockets than usual, left their fifty-cent tips, and headed home to put up the hurricane shutters.

A gun range outside Baton Rouge, Louisiana, had been packed all morning and was forced to hand out numbers for those waiting for a lane. By ten-thirty, they had to set fifteen-minute time limits of target practice to avoid a riot.

It almost worked.

And in a massage parlor along the I-75 corridor in Georgia, the scantily clad Asian masseuses had a run of last-minute needs to satisfy, while across the country in the Central Valley of California, below Sacramento, a Hispanic field worker told her friend that she was going back to El Salvador, "*Donde sea mas seguro.*"

"Where it's safer."

Only Connecticut saw no reaction, as that state had already outlawed gun ownership, and no one cared. Anyone who did had already left. So, Greenwich was as calm as any other weekday. Connecticuters were happy to have been early to the trough.

In the Oval Office, the television crew wrapped their gear as quickly as they could to get the hell out of Dodge. In less than a half-hour, the White House would feel like a graveyard at midnight.

Only less safe.

During that last surge of chaos, President Ed Navarro stepped over to a tall and handsome black man named Roger Pinkins—President-Elect Roger Pinkins—fifty-two, relaxed, sardonic.

"Thanks for leaving me with that," he said.

Navarro said, "Your people pushed it through. I just signed it."

"Now I get to deal with it."

"I'm sorry. I really am."

As Pinkins looked around at the receding madness, Ed Navarro asked him how the transition was going. "Terrifically," Pinkins said. "Your people have been gracious, efficient, and forthcoming. I had no idea it could go so well."

"Until this."

"Until this."

"CIA has filled you in on security issues to your liking?" Navarro asked.

"Couldn't be more thorough," Pinkins said. "As to my liking...."

He left it at that.

Navarro grinned and asked, "Learn anything new?"

"More than I wanted," Pinkins joked back.

"Every day," Navarro said.

"Well," Pinkins allowed, "I guess I knew that going in. Still," he admitted, "Daisy asks me every morning why I accepted when the DNC called and asked me to run."

Navarro chuckled. He knew the feeling and those questions well. That he had managed to stay married and only go a tad greyer was the major accomplishment of his life as he saw it.

Pinkins said, "Feel free to check in anytime."

To which Ed Navarro said, "I'll be sportfishing in Panama. Good luck." He shook hands — sincerely and warmly — and turned to leave, with, "I'll see you at the inauguration tomorrow — if security will let me in." He grinned again and left.

Relieved.

"Yeah," Pinkins said darkly as the last of the TV crew and Navarro's aides fled for cover. He caught a monitor with Wolf Blitzer saying, "Outrage in America: Guns are gone, but will gun owners go peacefully?"

Pinkins wanted to believe they would, but he — and he suspected Wolf — knew that was nigh to impossible. Maybe he wouldn't run for a second term.

Maybe there would be no country to run.

Chapter Four

The night before the inaugural ceremonies felt excruciatingly long in America. Countless shootings erupted across the land, mainly to inanimate objects — billboards supporting gun control, road-rage incidents having to do with unappreciated bumper stickers, and Democratic campaign offices, even though most of them had closed, post-election — but some four-hundred plus people were injured in multiple melees.

Miraculously, no deaths occurred.

In the following analysis, police would discover that nearly as many Democrats had guns as Republicans, something no one had ever suspected because no one had ever polled the folks who favored gun-control. The major difference was that Democrats generally had one or two guns "for protection," while Republicans had hundreds of guns and as many reasons.

Greater fury.

The inauguration turned out to be the least-attended in modern history other than 2021, with more police and military than attendees, it seemed — though it seemed likely that many of the "citizens" were plain-clothes cops and federal agents. So, there was no accurate count.

The new president was instructed not to get out of his limo and walk down Pennsylvania Avenue. He accepted the direction happily, and the opening ceremonies went without incident — for a few minutes.

As newly-elected president Roger J. Pinkins approached the podium to be sworn in behind tripled layers of bullet-proof glass — the Secret Service had decided to err on the side of caution; *way* on the side of caution — boos were heard rippling through the crowd. For, though Pinkins himself had not signed the proclamation, his party had pushed it through. Signs reading Death to Democrats! — with images of assault rifles — littered the crowd. Then they were gone, those protesters having been discreetly led away by no one knew who.

On the Capitol steps, Almost Ex-President Navarro, his wife and grown children, and the other living presidents — all but one noticeable exception (rumors raged that he was not invited) — sat in attendance, along with their family members. Pinkins' wife Daisy and their two teenage daughters stood proudly by.

Pinkins' running mate and new vice-president stood by close at hand with her husband and four grown children. Sarah "Sally" Hawkins smiled the same smile she had been smiling for the past two years on the long campaign trail. Their victory was hard won and close, not to mention hard to say — Pinkins-Hawkins did not roll off the tongue — with less than one-hundred-thousand votes separating them from their Republican challenger, Alfred Corzone, a wealthy industrialist with ties to the Communist Party.

That was what the commercials claimed.

In truth, Corzone was a centrist, not wholly opposed to the new anti-gun legislation, but not in favor of "the total

disarmament of America," as he put it. His "failure to stand strong against federal villainy and government overreach," and for "not defending the Second Amendment as it was meant to be," resulted in a failure to draw out staunch gun proponents, and he lost. Even he was surprised.

On Pinkins' side, Sally Hawkins had proved to be a worthy running mate. In debate after debate, she slayed Corzone's VP pick, an Iowa senator named Priestly, who just was not up to the job. Lazy and opinionated, he spewed easily debunkable "facts" as true when an average C-student in middle school could have answered the debate question correctly.

Priestly came into the race fully unprepared, ignorant of the law and history, and apparently apathetic to his own shot at being the first VP from Iowa since Wallace in 1941. All of this ran together to make him perhaps the worst male second-on-the-ticket Republican candidate in American history.

But Priestly was Corzone's "gun guy." So when Corzone would attempt to draw a centrist line on the threatened anti-gun laws, Priestly would come out the next day fuming and frothing at the mouth about the "alt-left's attack on our sovereignty" and "the unmitigated need for personal protective armament" and "Guns for ALL!"

He was also pro-life, anti-abortion, pro-death penalty and anti-immigrant—all the usual suspects rolled into one vice-presidential mouthpiece—but he had nothing else. Nothing. Having him on the ticket backfired spectacularly.

As it turned out, Americans were tired of the same old complaints and threats, the fearmongering, and the ongoing spate of shooting deaths over the past decades. America, as a nation, felt tired, worn out—if narrowly so. Enough for the Corzone-Priestly ticket to go down by 98,251 votes—only four in the Electoral College. Their last-ditch appeal went to the Supreme Court, but the justices politely asked them to go away.

Their familiarity with history exceeded his. They remembered every election since 2000 and refused to consider their case. "No standing," they said, the usual, inarguable brush-off.

Pinkins had chosen well with Sally Hawkins, a skilled orator with twin law degrees, one from Princeton and one from Yale, in criminal and constitutional law, respectively. Red state folks did not trust her, but whine as they might, she made sense to more voters than she alienated. Her Midwest vowels did not hurt.

Many said she "dragged Pinkins across the finish line." America had had one black president, and in many (white) minds, that was enough. One too many. But Roger Pinkins was calm and quiet, predisposed to campaign speeches that were short on fire but strong on understanding. He did not make his mark with policy so much as with honesty — a trait so rare that he won, if with Sally's Caucasianary assistance.

For all his college-educated blackness, Roger Pinkins understood working America — especially white America. He spoke tirelessly about programs to Get America Working Again by reviving the CCA and the WPA through scores of much-needed infrastructure projects, subsidized college and technical school "scholarships" for those unable to afford higher education on their own, and a somewhat radicalized healthcare overhaul "that just might work."

Still, there were those who "blamed" his success on his running mate — *don't give the black guy credit if you can help it* — and to be fair, Sally Hawkins was something else on the campaign trail. A career prosecutor turned international advocate, Hawkins was shrewd. She chose her clients carefully, always picking winners. Her defense of innocent women charged with self-defense-related homicides brought her national fame, which Sally turned into global acclaim when she defended three Pakistani women and one teenaged evangelical in a complicated case. The girl was raped, and the three Muslim women came to her defense, killing the rapist before he could kill the girl.

Now there was news cycle.

Even the far right was happy at their exoneration. They had to be. The white girl was the daughter of a prominent media-darling pastor from Ohio who had fought against birth control, abortion, Planned Parenthood, and religious freedom for thirty years, since high school. When his daughter was raped by an immigrant from Central America, then saved from death by three women in Burkas, he really had no choice but to get onboard, as did most of his followers.

When Sally Hawkins took the case—and won—she got right-wing cred the likes of which no one on the left had seen in decades. A lifelong Democrat, she happily accepted speaking engagements at Bob Jones University and Liberty University and Oral Roberts University and the rest—providing she controlled the topic and subject matter, pre-approved the questions, and was guaranteed ample press coverage. I.e., Sally Hawkins would only speak on matters related to the empowerment of American women, and she was good at it. She had it down.

She also had politics in mind for her future, in service of which she managed to cleverly merge women's rights with greater success for men in the workplace and out. She made convincing arguments that "keeping our women and daughters safe from crime" was the best thing men could do for themselves.

It was brilliant and worked like the charm she predicted. Sally rose through the mainstream media "faster than a whale fart in the deep ocean," as her husband Paul was wont to say. Roger Pinkins chose her without hesitation, brought her onboard before he had a campaign manager, and Sally Hawkins did exactly as he had hoped.

She helped him win.

Now she stood with her family, among the families of presidents past and the highest ranking members of both political parties in Congress — the ones who weren't too afraid to leave their home states or heavily-patrolled compounds — and smiled her smile. Though the mood was tense onstage, the projected tone was positive.

Everyone on the dais wore bulletproof vests under their overcoats.

Over the centuries, since 1789, Congress had changed the oath occasionally, switching things around here and there to suit the times. This year, they decided — for a reason no one knew or could understand — to have the new president sworn in first, as opposed to second, as had been tradition. Since Congress got to do what they wanted in this regard, the new order was set.

As Chief Justice Park Chun Hei stepped up to face Pinkins, a hush fell over the crowd. Apparently, there was some decency and respect for the peaceful transfer of power left in America. At least in Washington D.C. on January 20th.

Park smiled at Pinkins, who returned it, and Park said, somewhat playfully given the gravity of the oath and the prevailing instability in the country, "Shall we?"

Pinkins met his mirth. "Yes. We shall."

After another shared smile that reached back as far as those who could hear without amplification, Park and Pinkins moved to the microphone. The chief justice read his part to avoid "pulling a Roberts" and led, "I do solemnly affirm...."

Pinkins said, "I do solemnly affirm...."

"...that I will faithfully execute the Office of President of the United States...."

"...that I will faithfully execute the Office of President of the United States..."

"...and will, to the best of my ability...."

"...and will to the best of my ability...."

"...preserve, protect and defend the Constitution of the United States...."

"...preserve and protect—"

The first wave of shots rang out.

Well-trained and seasoned Secret Service agents dove onto everyone of importance, forcing them to the ground, covering them with their own bodies, as a full, well-rehearsed military response went into high gear. Previously hidden law enforcement of all stripes emerged from every nook and cranny like black ants from a hill.

More shots were heard, sounding like thousands of automatic rounds being fired, as inaugural attendees ducked and ran for cover. No one wanted another Las Vegas with a sixty dead and five-hundred wounded.

Times ten.

Despite the roiling chaos, the Secret Service performed brilliantly, as did every other agency involved in the response. They'd had practice a few years ago when they bungled that *other* situation badly. No shots were fired until officers were certain of their targets, and since no targets were spotted, no shots were fired.

Except by the "shooter," who remained untraceable.

As more bursts sounded and echoed around the many

edifices of downtown Federal Land, presidents—new and old—were shuffled away with their families and other dignitaries. Escape routes had been well-planned, pre-secured, and utilized to their highest efficiency. The new president was inside Marine One in less time than anyone could have imagined, especially him, and all six helos were up and roaring away before anyone on the ground had any idea as to the origination of the continued shots, which seemed to be coming from many directions at once.

Amazingly, no one was hit, no one was shot. No bullets took out windows or porta-potties—leading some on the ground to wonder if they were not responding to fireworks or blanks. Either way, in seconds, F-16s and F-22s roared overhead, making a strong visual statement about protecting the commander in chief. Seconds later, the sky crawled with them, zipping back and forth, low, overhead. How they avoided midair collisions was unimaginable, but the entire affair ended in less than four minutes. The president had been evacuated.

The nation was safe.

Chapter Five

In under thirty-minutes, two important events occurred.

One, the "gunfire," was determined to have been carefully placed large caches of fireworks. How the nine packages of "false ordnance" went undiscovered by anyone beforehand could not be explained.

A few heads did roll.

Two, in a SCIF deep inside the Pentagon, Chief Justice Park finished swearing in the new POTUS. Elsewhere, so as not to have both in the same room, even a SCIF, given the gun scare, Justice Ricardo Salon—whose name always sounded like a *nom de porn*—swore in Sally Hawkins to the vice-presidency.

Then a third thing happened.

As Pinkins was about to repeat his last line— "and will, to the best of my ability, preserve, protect, and defend the Constitution of the United States"—a woman in the room said, "Well, it's a little late for that."

Pinkins looked at her and said, "You're fired," then repeated his line. It was official: Roger James Pinkins was officially the new president.

The snarky woman, a holdover from the former administration known for her "forthright" manner, spluttered,

"But I'm secretary of agriculture. I'm ninth in line."

Pinkins said, "Not anymore."

Someone, a staffer, started to play "Hail to the Chief" on his phone, to which Pinkins said, "Can the music. Let's get to work." He walked out, and the entourage followed. Some were grinning; the rest were simply relieved to be getting on with it.

The secretary of agriculture was led off and left outside the front gate.

By the time President Pinkins returned to the White House, he had been given a full security update. The fireworks had been found, calm restored, no one was hurt, and an all-out search for the culprit(s) was underway. "Good news," he told his CIA head—another holdover who had served two administrations faithfully and was probably not going anywhere—and they all poured into the Oval Office.

Cameras were already set up as Pinkins had ordered. Though seemingly mild-mannered, he was no lollygagger. Roger Pinkins was a man of action.

"My fellow Americans," he said, looking through the teleprompter images into the lens. "As you know, I have inherited a difficult legacy. As a result, there is already some confusion in the streets."

For a man known for understatement, this one took the cake. Total pandemonium would have been a better descriptor.

The fireworks during the televised inaugural had cued the crazies who were ready and waiting and rushed out onto the streets in full force. Offending billboards were either now so full of holes they could not be read, or they had been set afire and burned to the ground. Store windows were shot out even if the shooters had no idea who was inside or their position on the new law. Road rage incidents increased a thousand-fold.

Gun nuts were going nutty.

In Minnesota, Alabama, California, and Maine, shouts of "Go ahead! Just try and take my guns, dammit!" were followed by the rapid waste of ammunition—ammo that others were hoarding for when they had to take a stand against the Deep State coming for their guns.

Pinkins warned viewers calmly but sternly, "We are forced to take immediate action on the bill signed into law just before I took office, titled the Gun Care Act."

Probably the worst false labeling in Congressional history.

Pinkins read, "GCA was brought to the floor of the Senate by Majority Leader Kingman in the last days of the former administration and passed fifty-one to forty-nine. From there, it went to the house, where it passed 218 to 214, with three abstentions. The law was challenged immediately, brought before the Supreme Court in a forced early session, and was upheld five to four."

Pinkins took off his glasses and said with great sincerity, "Fellow Americans, we are a nation of laws. We have survived as we have because we *are* a nation of laws. GCA is the law. All guns are now illegal in America. Let me say that again: All guns are now illegal in America. No guns of any type may be privately owned, be manufactured in the United States, or imported into our country. That is the law.

"As your newly elected president, I have sworn to uphold *all* laws of this land. And I will. That is my obligation unless and until this law is overturned. So I ask, as did my predecessor, President Navarro, that you all obey this law peacefully and orderly to make America the great country it once was, again. God bless this nation and its laws."

After the speech, newly minted vice president Sally

Hawkins waited for her new "boss" to be alone in a quiet corner and stepped close, keeping her voice low. "'Unless and until the law changes,'" she said, repeating his words. "Should we be offering false hope?"

Pinkins said, "If I won over a hundred people, I may have saved their lives."

Hawkins said, "There's going to be hell to pay, one way or another."

Roger Pinkins could not disagree.

But they were to awaken the next day to a surprise. Not that anyone had really listened to what Pinkins had to say or believed a word of it, but calm had come during the night. In towns and cities across America, peace prevailed. Not a car was out. Not a man, woman, or child.

Anywhere.

Once the stock-huggers had gotten the fire and fury out of their systems, they had apparently gone home and locked the doors, waiting to see what would happen next. Detroit felt like a ghost town again. Even New York City fell silent. Atlanta and Denver looked post-apocalyptic, the left behinds hiding behind closed curtains. Every theme park and attraction in America closed "until further notice."

Their stockholders demanded it.

In Lake Tahoe, a few brave young souls snuck onto the slopes and had it all to themselves. In Virginia, a rogue dirt track driver ran laps alone, whooping and hollering. In Cocoa Beach, a lone surfer could not believe his good fortune at the clean eight-foot winter swells he rode alone.

Life in America had simply stopped.

No one was happier than new president Roger Pinkins. Former president Nestor Navarro was already trawling off Bocas del Toro and could not have cared less. He had signed the law then left.

But not everyone was so detached.

CHAPTER SIX

Though the Millers had been in Big Angie's bunker for less than forty-eight hours, they were nearly suffocating and sweating like Fins in winter, only less happy about it. Twyla Miller said, "Anj, I can't take it anymore. I need me some air."

Before Angie could stop his wife, she was up and opening the door. Everyone but Eric followed her out. Eric said, "Sorry, Dad. Maybe you shoulda thought about the ventilation issue a little more when you built this thing."

Big Angie pouted angrily. "Had to do it all by myself."

"Dad, you wouldn't let any of us help. Hell, you didn't even tell us it was down here till it was done."

"S'posed to be a secret."

"It was."

"Make everyone safe."

"And we appreciate that. But we have to breathe. Sorry." That said, he went upstairs to join the others for iced tea and sandwiches.

When Twyla called down to let her husband know lunch was ready, he did not reply, choosing instead to open a can of potted meat and a box of hardtack while he checked the action on several of his guns.

An hour later, he was sweating like the Philippines and

came upstairs.

Twyla stood ready with a cool towel and a dry towel, and a tall glass of iced tea with fresh lemon. Big Angie wiped his wide face and round head with the dry one, drank half the glass of tea in one gulp, then passed guns out to everyone over the age of eight.

"We'll take turns standing watch," their patriarch said. "I'll go first—me and Eric. Eric, you take the back bedroom. I got the pitcher window. Twyla, you can stay in the kitchen—make food if you want. Just check out the side every few minutes. It's kinda tight back there, but an ATF guy or his dog could get through, and we'd be fucked."

Twyla said, "Thanks," hoping her husband wouldn't hear the sarcasm, and Erica said, "Dad. Language?" But the kids had not been listening. They were enjoying the weight of loaded weapons in their hands, the littler ones at their feet marveling upwards.

Angie moved on to greater things. "As official spokesman for the New Revolution—"

Eric cut in. "That was real smart of you, Dad. Getting out in front of it like that. Taking a position."

"Oh yeah, Pop," Ferdie said. "Your YouTube videos are through the roof. We got like a hundred thousand hits just this morning. Twitter's goin' crazy, too. You got like ten thousand hearts and shit. Retweets. I've never seen anything like it."

His father said, "Yeah, well, you two take care'a that social media crap. I've got my people doin' outreach. Knockin' on doors in twenty-three states. Fuckers."

Erica said, "Dad. Please."

Eric said, "Don't listen to her. You're a legend, Dad. Already. It's awesome."

Ferdie threw in, "Yeah. Just for tellin' the truth."

He said it, but he was wondering if he would still have a job when he showed up for work, and his liberal bosses found out what his father-in-law was up to—who he was and what he had become.

Angie went with it. "What the hell's happened to this country? We let it go to hell, that's what. We didn't speak up when we had the chance." Ferdie asked when that was, and Angie said, "Always! Nation'a pussies."

Erica gave up and left the room.

Eric said, "Well, you spoke up plenty, Dad."

"But where the hell was everyone else, huh?" Big Angie asked, riled.

Ferdie said, "Hiding in their corporate caves." Liking the sound of that, he added, "Caving in to pressure from the libtards."

Eric said, "Pussies."

Ferdie said, "Bitches," thinking more of his libtard lezbo bosses.

Angie said, "I was alone in this." He sounded like a sad thirteen-year-old. But then he rebounded. "But I was right, dammit!"

"Yeah, you were, Dad," Eric said. "You were brave."

Ferdie said, "And now it's gonna all pay off for you, Pops. We're gonna be rich. You just wait to see the hits we get later today. We'll be all over the fuckin' Internet. People in India will know who you are."

He made sure the battery on his iPhone was charged full-up.

Angie was not sure why his son-in-law was interested in what anyone in India would think of his stance on Second Amendment freedoms in fucked-up America, but he nodded with a sneer and a snarl. "This is just the beginning."

"We're gonna *kill!*" Eric said.

"We're gonna KILL!" Ferdie shouted, setting down his brand-new Ruger SR1911 and his Bushmaster XM-15—with a black-market bump stock—in order to wield two new iPhones.

"Yeah. We're gonna kill!" Eric yelled again, grabbing up his Smith & Wesson .45 and matching S&W M&P Sport AR with his own modified bump stock, waving them in the air like Zapata on back-alley human growth hormones.

Causing Angie to say, "Be careful with those, boys. They're loaded. We don't want anyone getting hurt."

"Of course not, Dad," Eric said, and lowered the guns to his sides, looking like a reprimanded pitiful, if well-armed, puppy.

Angie glanced around at his weaponized brood and made his decision. "Enough of this chitty-chat," he said, steeling himself for his next appearance on the world stage of American outrage. "Let's do this."

Eric agreed wholeheartedly. "Yeah! Let's *do* this! Let's get famous as fuck!" He took his place beside the front picture window, off to one side, ready. "Locked and loaded, Dad," he said with proud defiance. "Kids?"

His armed children took their loaded weapons—safeties off—and spread out around the house, strategically placed as previously instructed by Grampa.

In the kitchen, Twyla nervously twirled a dishtowel in her hands, certain that none of this could come to any good end. But Angie Miller was her husband, and he needed that knee surgery *bad* if he was going to work at anything ever again. If fame could bring in those extra bucks to cover what none of their insurance would—Angie had not had any for years; refused Obamacare on principle—then have at it.

"Just be safe," she called out from the kitchen as she picked up her Colt AR 15—dubbed "America's Rifle" by the NRA because…of course.

"AR. Get it?" Angie had said when he gave it to his wife as an anniversary present—paid for out of her salary. Gun in hand, Twyla peered out the kitchen window, seeing nothing but her trashcans and recycle bin, which gave her comfort for the moment.

When everyone was in place at their stations, Big Angie started for the front door. Stopping just short of it, he adjusted his own crisscrossed bandoliers, racked his Armalite M-15 A4—Angie was a purist—and his Colt .45—ditto—and nodded for Ferdie to open the door.

Ferdie set his Bushmaster on the side table by the front door where everyone dropped their keys under the wall of family pics, shoved his Ruger down the back of his cargo pants, glanced at Eric, who glanced at their father, and all three gave nods of support and determination, and Ferdie opened the door.

The crowd of field reporters and their camera people pressed forward in a wave. They had been waiting two days for Big Angie's appearance, speaking to their on-air anchors on the event in the push of anticipation.

"Gaither Cromier here at the home of Angelo Miller, where Mr. Miller has just stepped outside to speak with us."

"Angelo Miller is being accompanied by his son-in-law, Frederick Miller."

"Mr. Miller and his son are armed and ready, it appears, Sam."

"Are we safe here, Eddie?"

Then the questions started, all reporters shouting at once.

"Do you have a statement, Mr. Miller?"

"Are you angry, sir?"

"What is going to be your next move, Angie?"

"Over here, Angelo! Tell our viewers what you plan to do!"

Angie Miller muttered, "Don't call me Angelo," then held up his hands to get everyone to quiet down, forgetting that he was holding a loaded AR 15 and a .45.

Reporters yelped and ducked.

"Calm down, calm down," Angie said, lowering the guns. "This is just a press conference, not an execution. Nobody's gettin' shot yet."

He felt empowered, referring to what he was doing as a press conference.

Angie turned to twin-phoned Ferdie. "Are you getting all this?"

"Every bit, Pop," Ferdie said as he shifted for a better shot—an iPhone in each hand, one on his father-in-law and one on the crowd. "This YouTube video will *kill*!"

"Okay, good," his father-in-law said, and turned to the crowd. "Who's talkin' to me?" he wanted to know.

There had been a pool—ten dollars a pick—between the gaggle of reporters and Belle South, a black reporter from Memphis, had "won." She breathed in all the courage she could smell in the air, put away her abject fear of getting shot by a crazy white man, and stepped forward. "I am, sir. Belle South. WMC Action News."

"Okay," Angie said. "That a Fox station?" He did not recognize it.

"NBC affiliate, sir."

"Fake news," Angie said. "But go ahead. You won the pool." Then he asked, "Where's my money, by the way?"

The deal was that Angie Miller would get the full

proceeds in return for speaking to the press. A nervous P.A. got a nudge and skittered crablike, sideways as to present a narrower target, holding a wad of cash. "Here, sir," the frightened college kid said, and crabbed back.

"Thanks," Angie said, handing the money to Ferdie, who could not take it because both of his hands were full. So Angie stuffed his .45 in his belt, took the folded roll, and shoved it into his pocket.

He turned back to Belle South and said, "Whattaya wanna know? Could you bunch even decide on a relevant question to ask? One that ain't bullshit?"

"Yes, sir, I believe we have," Belle said diplomatically.

"Come on, come on," Angie baited her. "We got a new Revolutionary Civil War to get on with here." He wanted to make sure to cover all his bases. He racked the slide on his AR and fired a burst into the air.

For effect.

The result of the special show was that another single shot was heard, and Angie Miller took one to the head—dropped like a busted watermelon, instantly deceased.

"Pops!" Ferdie hollered, making sure to get a good video of *everything*.

Twyla's scream came from inside as Eric's eyes went wide, and he opened fire through the picture window, this being the cue for everyone else to follow suit.

Rapid fire came from every window in the house.

The fusillade of return fire seemed to come from everywhere at once, and in such volume that the house quickly looked like a special-effects bonanza in an A-list summer tentpole movie with an unlimited budget for squibs.

Only these were not squibs.

Reporters ran for their news vans and dove inside, Belle

South thinking that she had just gotten the scoop of her life and that she would forever be remembered for asking the question of Angie Miller the day he got shot on live television in front of his house as he was preparing a call to arms for his many wingnut Twitter followers.

News crews dropped their tall satellite antennas as quickly as possible and fled for their lives. One van did not get its pole all the way down before the driver took off, catching the expensive broadcasting arm on a low hanging tree limb, bending the antenna in half. The top fell to the pavement and threw sparks as the van sped away under a hail of embers from the power line that the limb caught.

A transformer exploded.

As agents from several branches poured out like ants from every nook and cranny in the already evacuated neighborhood — none of the Millers had noticed the preceding silence — Twyla and Erica, Allison and the kids all fired until they couldn't.

Until they were dead, too.

So much firepower poured into the Miller house that, in less than a minute, it collapsed, killing even the unarmed grandbabies.

Angie's war had officially begun in his absence.

CHAPTER SEVEN

On the watch floor in the situation room—really a cluster of rooms—intelligence officers watched the unfolding Gun Retrieval Crisis, as CNN was calling it, on a phalanx of media screens.

All was not well in America.

In the Surge Room, an actual room, President Roger Pinkins sat with his V.P. Sally Hawkins, Chief of Staff Henry Hillerman, DNI head Porter Clausen, Chairwoman of the Joint Chiefs of Staff Audrey Callahan, CIA Director Pat Clooney, National Security Advisor Dick Lingh, FBI Director Drew Parsely, ATF Director J. Carter Smith, and a few other higher-ups. The discussion was supposed to be about ways to proceed without too many deleterious effects on American life, but Angie Miller's "execution" had taken center stage.

That was what Sinclair News was calling it.

Pinkins paced, livid, encapsulating his ire in a single word. "Fuck!"

DNI head Clausen asked, "Do we have a body count yet?"

CIA head Clooney said, "Six adults, five children, two of them under three."

Pinkins repeated, "Fuck!" Then fleshed that thought out with, "What were these people *thinking*?"

VEEP Hawkins was her usual pithy self. "ATF or the Millers?" Pinkins threw her a look—a warning shot across her brow. She said, "You're taking away their freedoms, their right to arm themselves."

"Me?" Pinkins shot back.

"Welcome to the Revolution," Sally said. "We're the bad guys. The fascists."

Pinkins muttered at her, "Why did I pick you to be my running mate, again?"

"To be the voice of your conscience. Your inner guilt."

"I'd say I'm doing fine on that score all by my lonesome, thank you." He turned to his chief of staff. "Henry, options?"

Henry turned to the head of ATF Carter Smith.

Smith, a veteran public official of incredible calm, even at the relatively young age of fifty-two, said, "It's pretty much what we expected, sir."

Pinkins was not having it. "Who gave the order to kill that man and his entire family?"

"Congress, sir," Smith said. And he mimicked, "'It's the law now.'"

"I don't recall the law calling for the wiping out of an entire family in goddamn Akron—children, for fuck's sake."

"Those restrictions or clarifications were never made, sir," Smith said. Responding to Pinkins' flashing glare, he added, "The law calls for whatever extraordinary methods might be required to implement GCA. To quote: 'Any armed resistance will be met with extreme prejudice,' that generally referring to whatever firepower is available at the time."

"The man shot into the air," Pinkins said.

"The man shot," Smith said. "He fired his weapon before a group of some fifty or more press and 250 mixed law enforcement officers. They had no choice, sir."

"Yes, they had a choice!" Pinkins fired back. "Don't. Shoot!"

"Not an option, sir. Given the situation." Carter Smith held firm. Whether he agreed with the action or not, his job remained to uphold the law. Same as everyone else in the Surge Room.

Pinkins said, "Why on God's green earth were there 250 'mixed law enforcement officers' there to begin with? Isn't that a bit of overkill? So to speak."

He did not laugh at his own joke.

NSA head Dick Lingh felt the need to help his fellow officer Carter Smith. "Miller was all over the Internet bragging that if the law passed, he would personally wage a war on the U.S. government," Lingh said.

"He fired in the *air*," Pinkins said again.

Lingh said, "He claimed to have hundreds of thousands of followers ready to shoot any law enforcement personnel who came 'within a hundred yards' of their weapons, sir. He was serious, and his followers are serious. We had to take that threat seriously."

Pinkins said, "What you're saying is that you had to send a message."

"We did, yes sir," Smith said.

"Well," Sally Hawkins said. "I'd say it went out loud and clear."

Pinkins shook his head woefully. "And no doubt made any further attempts to enforce the law a hundred times more dangerous than it had to be."

The FBI head threw in, "Hard to make the enforcement of this law any more difficult, sir. To be fair."

Pinkins sighed. "I suppose so." Then he looked around. "But can we try to use a bit more judicial thought the next time?"

Smith said, "Should we wait for him to actually shoot someone, sir?"

"Don't be a smart ass. You know what I'm saying."

"Not really, sir. The man had two loaded weapons, had threatened to use them on the first law enforcement official he saw who asked him to turn in his guns, and he fired his weapon, endangering the lives of some three-hundred people — not including whoever might have been hit by falling lead. Sir."

"Tell me again why we had 250 in law enforcement there?"

"Merely as a precaution, sir," Smith said.

Pinkins groaned and shook his head.

Sally Hawkins threw in, "Too bad he didn't take out a reporter. That would have helped us a lot."

Pinkins said, "Can I fire you yet?"

"I don't think so," Sally said. "Not unless you fire yourself first. Then you could take me with you. But then I wouldn't be around to grant you a pardon. And you might need me for that before this is over."

Pinkins glowered, but Sally seemed perfectly delighted with the possible scenario.

Turning back to the many large screens, all muted but running hyperbolic banners about Revolution, Civil War, the murder of a civilian — *the end of civilization* — Pinkins took a breath and let go a depleting sigh. "So, this is how it begins."

"This is it, sir," Smith said. "And it's only going to get worse before it gets better."

"If it ever does," Lingh said. Everyone else stayed out of it.

President Pinkins took another slow look around the

room, one that made even the most seasoned public officials uncomfortable, and he said, "So, where do we go from here? What happens next?"

Carter Smith said, "I think you know, sir."

Pinkins knew too damn well.

FoxNews knew, too. At the top of the hour, average white guy Ansley Hopper and his gussied-up co-anchor Melania Cooper—on the Hopper-Cooper Report—made hay while their sun shone.

"Patriots aren't having it, Melania," Ansley said.

"No, they're not, Ansley," Melania affirmed.

"All around this once-great country, Americans are arming themselves—"

"Taking up arms," Ansley felt the need to correct.

"Taking up arms, yes," Melania felt the need to corroborate. "Taking up their many arms and preparing to defend their Second Amendment rights."

"Their Second Amendment rights that have been suspended," Ansley said.

"Fully suspended, and folks are mad as hell, and they aren't going to take it anymore," Melania chirped, totally missing the irony of what she was saying. She had never seen the movie, either. "This time, it's for all the marbles," she said, only adding to the garbled message with another bad movie tie-in.

A wrestling movie that she *had* seen.

Ansley added his two bits. "Well, they're not losing their marbles this time, Melania."

"No, they're not, Ansley. Not this time."

The screen cut to a field reporter, one Matt LeFevre, *Outside Birmingham, Alabama,* the banner read, along with, *Americans are mad as hell.* LeFevre stood on a sidewalk interviewing three white men in ski masks who appeared agitated.

Masked Man One: "There is no way we are giving up without a fight!"

Masked Man Two: "Fight to the death!"

Masked Man Three: "Fight to the death for Freedom in America!"

All Three Masked Idiots: "Death to America!"

And the yelling and firing guns into the air.

Matt LeFevre: "Back to you, Ansley and Melania."

In the studio, Melania looked impressed and said, "Wow."

Ansley said, "I think they mean it."

"I think they do," Melania said.

And Ansley said, "That's it for the Hopper-Cooper Report. Judge Angelina Domino is up next."

CHAPTER EIGHT

In the lonely high country of Colorado, far from the hoity-toity elite enclaves of Aspen and Vail, in the middle of an empty alpine meadow, two two-lane roads intersected, their macadam surfaces going out due north, south, east, and west in straight lines as far as the eye could see. Being Colorado, there was, of course, a bar—only a bar—with two pickup trucks parked outside.

Inside, the television was set to Fox as Judge Angelina Domino came on to decry the new law and everything else non-ultra-conservative or Caucasian, her show's slogan, "We're so far right, it's wrong!"

They joyously celebrated their lack of inclusion daily.

The Four Corners bartender, a hard-edged mountain woman named Joline, squinted at the screen. "I hate that New York bitch. Ain't even a real judge," she said to the only patron in the place, who said, "Ain't even a real New York bitch. She's from Jersey." Which made Joline snort once and cough twice.

Joline then switched channels to MSNBC, where the caramel-toned female anchor was wearing a headscarf. Which led Joline to issue her common refrain, "To Hell in a handbasket." Which always made her lone patron grin.

David Billows did not hail from the high country but had taken the mountain solitude as providence, he said, and was determined to stay his course. "Cities have nothing for me anymore," he said to anyone who asked of his past, which he said included the rugged but wet and cold Pacific Northwest, the isolationist but hot and humid Deep South, with a stint in the army in between— "four years in Haji Hell." He also claimed several "escapes" from liberal enclaves like Taos, San Francisco, and D.C. His parlance was appreciated in the Colorado high country.

If pressed, Billows had horror stories about Los Angeles and Boston as well, though details on either were skimpy. "If you like 'diversity,' then those are your places," was about it. He called Montana "the antidote."

Billows often said he was "reformed," though he never said from what. At forty-five, his claimed age, he appeared ten years younger—like a newscaster. But if anyone looked closely, the signs were there—the lines, the tired eyes; but more often the flash of judgment from behind a tight squint, the kind that came along with age—and "Goddamned ear hair," as he once said to Joline to get a rare laugh from her.

David, never Dave— "Call me Dave I'll have to shoot you" —carried full armament wherever he went these days: a Glock 22 .40 15+1 on his hip, a Glock 43 9mm with standard clip on his ankle, a big chromed Taurus Desert Eagle .50 cross-draw shoulder-holster for show, a BCM RECCE-16 Mod, the Rolls Royce of ARs, and a strapped 12" Bowie blade for backup. "Loaded for rhino" was how Joline described him to anyone who asked—when he wasn't around. "Never seen a man carry more hardware," she'd say—and that if he ever fell in Summit Pond, he was a goner. "Sink like a nickel-plated rock."

Joline muttered something about either the shawled newswoman or the same clip Fox had shown with the three masked American "patriots" yelling "Death to America!" Sometimes with Joline, it was hard to tell exactly what bothered her the most, as everyone and everything seemed to get her goat at one point or another.

Every day.

The Arab-American anchor said, "Of course, this brings to mind another war and another time that worked to the detriment of the American empire. But make no mistake, America is at war again...this time with itself."

Joline could mutter no longer. She muted the TV and turned to David. "You tell me what in fucking good hell some goddam Al Kayta-reject bitch in a turban knows about war in fuckin' America."

With the television sound off, they could now hear the latest country and western patriot caterwauling on the local AM station.

Joline said, "I'll tell you goddamn what: that Muslim cunt comes in here, and she's seein' the business end'a Betty." Joline patted her own AR—a Delton DT Sport Lite because it was the cheapest she could find—lying on the bar within easy reach. She named it Betty after her favorite Rottweiler that had to be put down after biting a "goddamned hippie hiker," who got lost and stopped at her trailer to ask directions back to the trail.

David said, "I think you're safe here, Jo."

"Shit," Joline Weatherman said. "Ain't no one safe in this whole goddamn country. Not no more."

"I meant from her," David said, nodding up at the TV lady.

"Fuck her," Joline said, reaching peak rile earlier than

usual for a weekday. "Did you see what happened to that Angelo Miller guy and his whole goddamn family in his own goddamn house?" David said he had seen it. Then he sipped his beer without further comment. Joline said, "You sayin' it don't bother you? He had it comin'?" A blend of rising ire and astonishment crept into her words.

David grunted and said, "Let's just say he was outspoken."

Joline hollered to the high rooftops. "Well, fuck yeah, he was outspoken! Someone had to be! We got a right to our goddamn guns, David! What? Are you goin' liberal ACLU pussy on me here, snowflake? Am I gonna hafta shoot *you*?" She had her hand on her gun.

David said, "Not if I shoot you first," tilting his head with a gleam in his eye.

Joline squinted.

David said, "How about another draft?"

Joline lit a Marlboro and said, "Sure. You're the only one in the county brave enough to come in and keep me company. Middle'a the goddamn day, and every loudmouth within fifty miles cowerin' behind his couch waitin' for ATF to knock on his door so he can say 'Come on in, *sir*. Take my guns, *sir*. I don't mind, *sir*. Jus' don't shoot me, please, *sir*.'" The last part was Joline's attempt to sound like a possibly gay man giving up his purse poodle.

How she saw it in her mind.

Disgruntled with the caving in of real men in America, Joline grabbed the Bud Lite tap and drew a draught for David. She set it down in front of him with her characteristic flair and said, "On me."

David said, "Hell no, Jo. If I'm the only one buyin', then I'm the only one payin'." And with one slug, he poured down the entire beer. Then he burped, stood, put a fiver on the bar,

picked up his BCM AR, and walked out for his 1996 Ford
F-250 in the uncrowded parking lot.

Even Joline had to admit: "I like the way that man drinks
a beer."

Kinda made her damp.

CHAPTER NINE

After a stop at the "local" grocery store, fifteen miles out of his way, David Billows returned home— "home" being a compound at the end of a lonely road, at the end of a box canyon, at the end of time, it seemed. No powerlines, no cable, no cell reception. Only the occasional satellite.

Peacefully quiet by a flowing stream, the place could have been a Zen retreat except for the accoutrements—two well-constructed gun towers on either end of the front fence—ten feet of chain link topped with triple coils of razor wire. No one was manning the towers, but two armed men languidly paced the gate, letting David in without an undercarriage check.

The inner gate sat off-center in a tall and solid wall constructed of whole trees, spiked at the top and covered with more concertina wire, making it look like a cross between Fort Boone and the Road Warrior's gasoline fortress. Two more guards—one male, one female—waved him through.

After parking in the designated area—the fort had been laid out in an organized fashion, with five smallish cabins surrounding a central house/meeting space—David gathered his six bags of groceries and headed inside the main building.

For a compound, the place would have seemed

unremarkable to an outsider. It had no steel barricades or gun slots in the walls, no trip wires or hidey-holes, no machine gun emplacements—no bunker feel as all fortifications appeared to be on the outside.

The main room of the central hall felt downright homey, with comfortable furniture, curtains, and hand-hooked rugs. The floors were not poly'd but smooth, no doubt sanded for days when installed. The ceilings were wood, the walls were not. Construction was basic but appealing. Art hung on the walls—some of the pieces damned interesting—along with a few stuffed deer heads.

That was where the amity ended. Fifteen heavily armed survivalist types sat around the room playing cards, reading gun magazines, or playing with the five children, aged six to fifteen, two of them mixed race, the rest white. Everyone else was white except for one black woman, Marjorie, and a Hispanic man, Carlos. Beards were popular with the men, braids with the women, jeans and T-shirts with everyone.

David set the six plastic bags on the long counter—a single, fifteen-foot-long slab of Colorado pine, slick on the top, rough on the sides, bark intact, and nearly three feet wide—that ran the length of the kitchen.

"I stopped by Branson's," he said. "Shelves were pretty picked over. No jerky."

Groans went around the room, and Carlos said, "I don't know what the truckers are afraid of. Nobody's gonna shoot *them*. We all need to eat."

The guy with the longest beard, Arthur—everyone called him Mountain Man—said, "Nobody knows who's gonna shoot who. That's the problem."

Another guy with a slightly shorter beard, Al, said, "Most of them are probably better armed than we are."

Everyone laughed.

David kissed Marjorie on the lips gently—a peck—and said, "Kids seem to be adjusting."

Marjorie said, "They miss going out to play." She meant outside the fence.

"Well," David said philosophically—hopefully: "It shouldn't be too long. Just until it's safe."

Al said, "And that's gonna be never."

Mountain Man said, "Never's a long time, Al. 'Bout as long as until you find another woman willin' to marry you."

Everyone laughed again, and Al said, "At least I prefer women."

To which Mountain Man said, "I'll take that as a gay joke and take it out on you in your sleep. Watch out!"

He yelped, and Al jumped. "Not funny," Al said.

"Pretty funny," the oldest boy, Justin, said.

Marjorie looked at her two mixed-race girls and said to David, "I wish they were yours."

David said, "We all wish a lot of things these days."

An old woman, Denise, looking like a throwback to Haight-Ashbury in her tie-dye, came out of a back room with a mop and bucket and said, "I wish my back would stop hurtin' so I could proposition Al."

Al said, "Aw, you're too young for me, Mabel," and everybody laughed again at how Al was the only one who could get away with calling Denise "Mabel."

Denise said, "Well, be on alert. If Mountain Man don't getcha in yer sleep, I might." She tickled his ribs on her way past and outside.

"Always the tease, Mabel! Never the bride," Al called out after her.

Denise flipped him off as she exited the front door to

empty her bucket and get fresh water from the stream that ran through the corner of the compound.

Carlos said, "I heard Denise has the hots for Joline, down at Four Corners."

Mountain Man laughed. "Good luck with that," he said. "Joline's straighter'n the Seaboard Air Line."

"What's that?" Justin asked.

"Rail line between Wilmington and Hamlet, back home." Mountain Man originally came from Rocky Mount, one of the flattest spots in North Carolina—altitude ninety-eight feet. But he fancied himself a "higher altitude type."

Al said, "You would know."

He was not talking about Arthur's knowledge of rail lines.

Mountain Man said, "I'm tellin' ya. Watch yer backside tonight."

And everyone laughed one more time, until David said, "So, how we gonna kill this president?"

All laughter stopped.

"Not possible," Al said.

"Everything's possible," David said, and left it at that.

Word came in from a back room, "Satellite's up, anyone's interested."

Marjorie was, so she uncovered the small flat screen and turned it on, making sure the wires were hooked up properly this time. She had worked IT for almost two decades in D.C. and knew her shit when it came to telecom bullshit.

That was how David put it when bragging on her.

The screen came up as a live press conference was taking place in the White House. Press Secretary Cal Worthing, a loud and flamboyant man for the job, listened to a setup by a CBS reporter, Drew Costly. "Cal, the president has always opposed gun control, one of the only guys in his party to do so—certainly the only one to come out of a Democratic primary having said that."

Cal joked, "He's proud of that, by the way," getting chuckles from the press corps.

Drew went on to ask, "As the first Democrat to hold office in sixteen years, how does he feel about implementing GCA, and how is he dealing with the blowback he is getting from his own party?"

Worthing said, "He's the president, Drew. He didn't get there by being namby-pamby. That's an official term, by the way."

Someone in the back muttered, "How many 'by the way's' are we going to have to hear today?"

Cal heard her and said, "I'm just getting started."

Considering the tension in the nation, cajoling and counter-cajoling had remained a part of the daily press briefing with Worthing, something everyone in the room appreciated, even if it sometimes took him a while to get to his point.

He now said, "Look, as you know, the president swore to uphold *all* the laws of this nation, not just the ones he likes or members of his party prefer. He has made it clear that he will do just that. Rich?"

He turned to another reporter, but CBS's Drew Costly cut in, saying, "Follow up, Cal. What about Senators Blank and Crossley? House Speaker Cornwall? I mean, Republicans have finally, somewhat remarkably, retaken the house, and, as I hear it, they're not real happy right now."

Cal chuckled. "I'd say that's the understatement of the week—and it's been a helluva week vis-à-vis hard line statements."

The room agreed.

"But look," Cal went on, "and this little bit is off the

record," he winked. "Speaker Cornwall is between a rock and a shit storm, let's face it. But so is the president. Any way he goes on this, it's going to get him in trouble with the other side. As you know, POTUS ran on a bipartisan platform, and it is his greatest wish to keep his promises—despite those who want to derail him before he gets to week two. But the law is the law, and members of his party in the last Congress passed this law. GCA will be upheld, and its provisions will be prosecuted fully and fairly unless or until the law is changed. It's as simple as that. This president believes in the rule of law and will do nothing to make that inviolate."

A reporter from Fox, Andrea Corker, said, "Nice word, Cal, but will he follow up on that promise?"

"I just said he would, Andrea," Cal said, and turned to the senior black reporter in attendance. "Rich, you wanted to get in here?"

Rich Parsons, a veteran of the room for three decades, now an urban radio regular, said, "Yeah, Cal. Thanks. What's troubling to me is whether this law is even legal. It passed, sure, but there are already dozens of lawsuits in the works. I just don't see how it will stand the test of time and jurisprudence. So, why not cut off the problem at its head?"

"What's your question, Rich?" Cal said, indicating that he might be moving towards an adjournment for the day.

Parsons said, "I'm just wondering why the president doesn't take action on his own if he doesn't like this GCA thing. He could rescind it through a signing statement."

"That is not going to happen, Rich. The stakes are far too high to resort to a signing statement. This is likely to end up before the Supreme Court—"

"Again," Rich Parsons said.

"Again," Cal agreed. "And your point is well-taken.

Their decision was five to four, and it stands as law. For the president to buck, that would undoubtedly mean a polar plunge in his polling numbers, and God knows what extra chaos in the streets. Not gonna happen, Rich. If GCA is going to be repealed, it is only going to happen through action by Congress. That means a majority in the House and a super-majority in the Senate. Now, that is possible over time. But in the immediate? Not gonna happen. We are a nation of laws, and this is the law, and we need to rock-n-roll with it for the time being. And hey, maybe it will work out, and America will be better for it. That was the hope of the bill's sponsors, a hope shared by most in the president's party, and a few across the aisle — oh, and a large percentage of the American public, by the way." Worthing got the laughs he sought and wrapped up with, "Truth is, even if a new bill came to his desk, I doubt that the president would sign it."

Andrea Corker perked up. "You're saying that the president of the United States would veto any new law, any attempt to undo this unpopular law that was passed with a bare majority in Congress, and is extremely unpopular with the American public."

Cal Worthing did not miss a beat. "I'm guessing there was a question in there somewhere, Andrea, but let me say this. I won't accede to 'extremely' unpopular; we're talking less than two points, and that was after the fact. But here's the thing: this president did not run for office to be a punching bag or to go against the wishes of the American public writ large. But he *did* run promising to be unbiased in his opinions and, as much as possible, to forge a bipartisan relationship with both sides in Congress, with the ICA, and with the American public writ large. Beyond that, what can he do? He is bound by law, by his oath of office, and by his conscience — which by the way, I can personally attest is large, forceful, and honest. That's all. Have a good day, folks."

Worthing turned to leave but was caught by a last hollered question by Cecily Porter from CNN. "Cal, we've heard that the administration is going to start collecting guns in the northeast cities where they're less likely to meet resistance like in the South or other red states. Can you comment on that, please?"

Cal returned to the mike to say, "GCA is the law of the land, all of the land, in all of the states. No state is exempt, and none are preferred for one reason or another."

Cecily pushed. "Your answer is?"

"My answer is that we will be collecting all weapons, everywhere, as the new law prescribes. Thank you."

And he left.

CHAPTER TEN

As America is a large country, not every nook and cranny could be excised of weaponry on the first round. But the newly formed GCA coalition of essentially every law enforcement group in the nation did their best. Named the Special Agency for Firearm Eradication—SAFE—the men and women felt a part of something important and approached their work with the full dedication and determination they thought it deserved.

Most of them.

A large contingent of Second Amendment Rights activists still inhabited the station houses and federal agency offices of a gun-loving America. And there were problems. Some cops quit. Some refused to follow the order, the law. Some pretended not to see guns when they saw them and walked away, leaving citizens—usually friends, or at least friendlies—still armed. Some were simply unconvinced of the wisdom of going into someone's house and demanding their guns.

Some moved to Idaho.

But for the most part, the initial sweeps went smoother than expected. Most Americans complied—some begrudgingly, with words to express their displeasure—but surprisingly, few were hostile or ultimately resistant. Everyone braced for the worst, but — at least at first — the worst did not happen. The worst being an all-out gun battle on a crowded street in a major city.

Which was, in keeping with the reporter's question, where SAFE started. The decision had not been made, however, on the lessened likelihood of conflict but was simply a matter of numbers. More people, more guns — concentrations of both, not caution, made cities the kick-off points for the Ungunning of America, as it quickly became known.

To show that he believed in his mission and that it was safe, ATF Lead Agent Carter Smith led the first "entries — he refused the use of the word "raid" as certain "news" organizations screamed on an hourly basis — personally knocking on doors, being first to enter the premises, giving on-site interviews, even allowing angry citizens to vent on camera to him before asking them if they had been treated politely and with respect for their persons and property, etc. To which they had to admit, also on camera, that aside from losing their prized guns and being generally annoyed by that, the whole thing was surprisingly *not* unpleasant.

Then, on to the next house.

This standard operating procedure was occurring in every major city, sometimes one block at a time, sometimes an entire neighborhood if it was known, or anticipated, to be particularly gun heavy or more dangerous than other areas.

Beverly Hills was a breeze.

But in South Boston, Agent Smith expected trouble. He hoped things would not escalate beyond controllability, but he had his doubts. Still, he needed to make his point, that being, "We are coming for your guns; there's nothing you can do about it. We are legally empowered to employ a show of strength equal to the needs of any situation, but we will not be rude or pushy or threatening if you cooperate — no promises if you don't."

Carter Smith knocked on the first door and was greeted by the wife — a woman in her late fifties named Irene McKennon. It was immediately clear to Agent Smith that Mrs. McKennon had led a harder life than some — most, perhaps — but that, perhaps because of that, she would not be a problem. Her husband might be a different story.

Mrs. McKennon said to Mr. Smith, "I can guess what you come for."

"Yes, ma'am," he said.

"Well, might as well come in. Get it over with."

Smith went in alone. He found Mr. McKennon sitting in his La-Z-Boy, watching Angelina Domino ranting about GCA agents "running amok all over our sacred Constitution." Otherwise, the name on his chair matched his attitude.

"Ain't gettin' up to help you do your dirty work," McKennon said without looking at Carter.

"That's fine, Mr. McKennon," Carter said.

"Yer gonna hafta find 'em on yer own, as well. I ain't helpin'. No way."

"That's fine, sir. We can do that. We'll have to bring in the dogs, sir. Is anyone allergic?"

"Just to cops and freedom snatchers," McKennon said, laughing at his joke, his yellowed wife-beater bobbing.

"I understand, sir," Smith said, and signaled for the sniffing dogs.

Three agents with K-9s came in, the dogs whining and pulling at their leashes, eager to earn their keep. One went straight to a hall closet and gave a single bark to alert. The Kevlar'd agent opened the closet and easily found the shotgun and ammo.

Another agent led his K-9 upstairs, where the dog alerted him to a dresser, a nightstand, and the bedroom closet. That agent found a snub-nosed .38, an army-issue .45 from WWII, and a hunting rifle with a full clip. All the guns were loaded; none had been locked up or were outfitted with trigger locks.

Mrs. McKennon quietly told Carter Smith, "Tell the truth, glad to have 'em outa the house." Her "thank you" was unstated but clear. Mr. McKennon heard and grunted, but that was it.

Carter Smith thanked them both for their cooperation and encouraged them to have a nice rest of their day. Mr. McKennon's eyes never left his television screen and the agents left.

The next house was not as easy. A teenage boy ran from the home, making a break for it. He did not get far before waiting agents had him on the ground, knee to his neck, cuffs on his wrists, searching, and finding....

A video game.

Smith bent down. "That's it?"

His agent nodded. The kid was clean, otherwise.

"Son," Carter Smith said gently, "what the hell are you doing?"

"It's got guns in it!" the kid shouted, squirming. "It's a gun game! It's my favorite!"

Smith told the agents to let him up and uncuff him. Then he said to the boy as he was being helped up and released, "What's your name, son?"

"Tommy."

"Well, Tommy, I've got good news and bad news."

"Sir?" The kid looked ready to cry, certain he was going to prison for evading arrest — or something.

Smith said, "The good news is we don't give a rat's ass

about your video game, okay?"

Tommy had to look to see that the agent was being nice, kidding him a bit. "Okay," he said, still unsure of his crime. An agent handed the game back to him. He felt compelled to explain. "I heard on the news that they was takin' everything had to do with guns. Not just guns."

"Just guns," Smith said.

"And ammunition," another agent added. "Some peripherals and the like."

Smith shot the agent a look, and he stepped away.

"Oh, okay," Tommy said. "What's the bad news?"

Lead Agent Smith nodded toward the kid's front door where his mother was standing, left eyebrow up to her hairline, fuming.

Tommy saw his mother and said, "Oh shit."

"You're free to go," Carter said.

"Do I have to?" the kid said.

Smith nodded, and Tommy dragged up onto his mother's porch, where she immediately grabbed him by the ear and dragged him inside—after she broke the video game and threw it out on the lawn.

The agents had already searched her house—it was clean—and were moving on to the next one. Smith chuckled. "It's a bitch being dumb," he said.

"Being young," another agent said.

"Same thing," Carter said, and they all agreed.

The Chinese herb shop on the corner was easier. The owner—he had to be a hundred and twelve—nodded respectfully from behind his two-gallon glass elixir bottle filled with bathtub gin and nine small rattlesnakes from eighty years ago. He assured the agents that he had no guns and produced his weapon of choice. "Louisville Slugger," he said proudly and showed them how it worked. Moving like a man a fifth his age, he did a roundhouse Kettukari swirl, perfectly landing his end pose and smiling. The agents smiled back, and everyone left happy.

In the church next door, they did find a loaded revolver hidden in the pulpit. The minister smiled wanly. It was a bad neighborhood. Now he would have to rely on God.

Most of the houses that day were gun free, and the owners happily acceded to a search. Nothing to hide, nothing to lose. A few folks hurriedly put their weed away, then panicked when they saw the dogs. But the dogs had not been trained to find pot, just gun oil and powder.

Plastics.

Plus, the SAFE teams had clear instructions: no arrests for ANYTHING other than resistance to giving up weapons. If the agents came across a crime in progress, they could detain perps until local could be summoned, but they had no authority to arrest anyone for any crime other than refusing to surrender their weapons—not even for hiding them or refusing to say they had them or tell where they were.

The K-9s took care of all that.

Surprisingly to the SAFE agents, most gun owners did not seem to mind the process. They often thanked the agents for being professional, even for removing the weapons for them, and showed them out with a smile. Many said things like, "I didn't need it anyway," or "I won't miss it," or "Hell, I haven't had it out of the safe in ten years or more." Occasionally someone would say something like, "Well, okay. But if I get robbed tomorrow, you're gonna hear about it."

To which Carter Smith would say, "I'm sure I will."

Then he put the confiscated weapons in the thick metal tank on the SAFE trailer—originally designed for bomb disposal — and moved on to the next house, where hopefully no one would have a gun to begin with. In most cases, that turned out to be the case. So SAFE ran a mostly smooth and uneventful operation.

Though there were the occasional idiots.

Agents in one township discovered a pair of legs poking out from a small crawlspace opening and, when they dislocated the overly chubby man from his hole, found an enormous cache of automatic and semi-automatic weapons stashed under the floor joists. He had not had time to wrap them for protection, so they were dirty, which bothered the ATF guys more than the big guy's efforts to obfuscate his "collection."

He had shouted, "Don't shoot! Don't kill me! I'm unarmed! Don't kill me! Please! Don't shoot! I'm not armed!" Just somewhat obese and extremely stupid.

A female agent admonished him. "That's no way to treat a fine weapon like this," she said on seeing the high-quality AR, a $2,000 Daniel Defense V7 jammed with dirt.

The man said, "I know," and went hangdog on her.

Another agent told him he was "free to go."

The tatted-up fat man was confused and said, "But what about my outstanding warrants?"

The agents stopped, stared, shook their heads, and called local, who came and took him in on seven outstanding warrants for B&Es, assault, armed robbery, and domestic abuse. He sat in the back of the squad car beating his head against the Plexiglas panel, saying over and over: "Stupid, stupid, stupid, stupid, stupid."

The agents were still shaking their heads over beers later.

Later still, a nighttime action across town into a suspected MS-13 "safe" house caught everyone asleep and unawares.

Five heavily tatted men and "their women," along with six children, were packed into the two-bedroom frame house at the end of a street lined tightly with row homes. How the agents got to the last house without being noticed was a surprise to everyone on the street—right after they were surprised with their own entries.

SAFE officers led the bleary-eyed gangbangers and their families out into the cul-de-sac in their underwear and lingerie, gave them blankets, and told them to wait while the agents pored over every inch of the rental house, coming up with enough weapons to start a small army. They left dozens of knives.

As the group awaited arrest, they watched with sadness as Carter Smith and his crew dropped all the guns into the bomb trailer, being sure to let the gangstas know that all the guns would be crushed and smelted. "Turned into church bells," one of the more religious agents told them.

"Yeah, I heard they send them down to El Salvador to ring out freedom," another said, just to rub it in.

When Carter Smith told them all to "Have a nice rest of your night," one of the men looked shocked. "You're... leaving?" he said.

Smith said, "Unless you have something to tell us about the use of any of these weapons in any unlawful crimes or have some other confessions you'd like to make. We can call BPD if need be."

The men and women and children of this local MS-13 chapter looked at each other, knowing well that they had reams of confessions available, but chose to shake their heads no.

"Good then," Smith said. "Like I said, have a nice rest of your night."

With the remainder of the street having been checked and "relieved" of all weapons, the SAFE agents pulled away "with a full can," as they had come to say of their storage device.

Surprise was not always necessary; but rather, care and listening skills.

Two blocks over, several of Smith's SAFE agents had gathered at the front gate of a rundown house with junk in the yard and a high fence, behind which a small pack of foaming Rottweilers snapped at the air between themselves and the agents in black. Kevlar could not protect the agents from yellowed incisors, so they talked first.

"Sir, do you have any guns inside?"

The dogs' owner, a Viet Nam vet pushing seventy-five and looking worse for the years of PTSD, alcohol, drugs, and general declining health, said, "What the hell I need a gun for? I got *them*."

On the last words, the dogs seemed to understand that was their cue to unleash another fusillade of hurling drool and generalized canine viciousness toward the agents.

Their master told the agents, "I wouldn't come through that gate, I was you."

The SAFE group leader, a stout woman named Ellie Garcia, said, "Sir, can you please put the dogs away so we can come in and check? It's just our job is all."

The man seemed to respect that, but he remained wary. "Ya ain't gonna kill 'em, are ya?"

"No, sir," Ellie said. "We do not wish to harm you or your dogs." Then she added, "But I don't want my people harmed either."

The old vet thought a moment, then gave a single sharp whistle, and all five Rotts spun and ran into a pen with a top. When their owner clicked a remote, there followed a beep, and the gate closed automatically, locking the dogs in.

He told the agents, "Okay, I reckon. Just don't hurt my dogs."

"I promise we won't, sir," Ellie Garcia said. "We'll be in and out before you know it."

She opened the gate, and her team walked through and into the man's house. As she passed the grizzled ex-army grunt, Ellie said to him, "Dogs are a good idea, sir. Very effective against intruders—a good way to dissuade them in the first place. I expect you haven't had an unwanted visitor since you got those Rotts."

"Not a one," he said.

"Do you have any firearms in here, sir? It's easier if you lead us to them to start."

The man shook his head and let go a phlegmy laugh. "Shit," he said. "I ain't had a gun in my hand since 1972 when I left the goddamned army. Don't want one, neither. I like dogs. And they like you back."

"I can see they do," Ellie said, marveling at how the dogs sat in a silent line, eyes on their master, awaiting their next command—one that he did not have to give.

He had no guns in the house.

On the next street over, a tall and seemingly gentle black man with a wife and two kids mentioned the MS-13 problem in the neighborhood as a reason to keep his 9mm. Smith explained that much of that problem had just been relieved. The man said, "But what am I supposed to do if I need that back?" His 9mm. "If I need to protect my family?"

Carter Smith said, in his typically genuine way, "I understand, sir. But we are not authorized to give advice on personal defense."

"Yeah, yeah," the guy said with irritation, maybe not so

gentle after all. Or maybe he was just scared.

Either way, Agent Smith said, "Sorry for the intrusion." He made sure the 9mm got dropped in "the tank," and the agents left. No real resistance, no super hotheads, no shots fired — all in all, a good day and night's work.

But this *was* the city. Limitations on resistant activities were mostly curtailed by the close quarters, leaving no room to hide or paths of escape with so many agents dispatched to each neighborhood beforehand. Wide open red states would be more of challenge, where entire families sat defiantly in lawn and beach chairs in their front yards with their guns in their laps, beers in their hands, and the Stars and Stripes flying.

Some even played the song.

CHAPTER ELEVEN

One of the brassier Fox news hens peered out through her lush eyelashes into the camera and said, "The federal government estimates they have already confiscated some thirty-seven-million guns in just five days of what they call 'legal' searches. By the NRA's own estimates, this leaves some 360-million more guns to be located." She seemed to be scowling, perhaps because the NRA was running on fumes.

There came a loud *bang!* in the Four Corners Bar, and the television went dark, followed by several groans.

Joline Weatherman let go of a verbal fusillade. "Goddammit, Hepburn! That's the third TV this week! You ain't got no more in the park, do you? That was it."

The old timer with the smoking Colt Frontier .45, who looked like an extra from *High Sierra*, but in color, hung his shaggy bearded head so that no one could see his defiant rheumy eyes beneath his dusty brim. He shook "no" so slightly that only the regulars who knew him could notice.

Joline chastised him further. "Killin' TV sets don't make the news go away, old man." Then she turned to the others—business had picked up after the first week of "gun huntin' in America"—and asked who was "gonna cover for him this time?"

A young cowboy named Jason Biggers spoke up. "I will, Aunt Jo. You can have mine. I'll go get it." He finished his warm Lite and started for the door, passing the TV-killer on his way out. "And Hepburn," he said to the old coot, "leave that damn iron at the door next time, okay?"

Hepburn raised his head. "The hell you say, boy! Goddamn cold dead hands is how I see it!"

Joline had had enough. "All right, that's it. You're banned. Go on. Get out. Go *on*, now! And take yer damn arsenal with ya." She drew herself a rare early draught. "Don't come back packin' again. Like the old days in here, all over. Gotta draw the line."

"The hell you say, woman!"

"Hepburn," Joline said with minimal patience, a long slug of cold Coors soothing her before it even got to her stomach to do its work, shook her head as if fed up with a rowdy child. Softer, she said, "Go on, now. Go home and sleep it off."

The old codger grumbled and spat on the floor, eliciting another head wag from Joline. But he staggered over to retrieve his five other guns, hastily hung in disarray on the winter coat rack by the door.

Joline warned him, "Hep, just walk on home, now. You're too drunk to drive."

As he went out the door, the old man shouted, "Ain't too drunk to shoot, though!" And he shot up...something outside.

Everyone hoped it was not their pickup.

Though the broadcast had been interrupted at the Four Corners Bar just outside Nowhere, Colorado (and "Proudly!" so), elsewhere fans and haters stayed glued to their tubes, waiting for the next startling development in what had become the largest-scale law enforcement operation America had ever seen. Coverage ran non-stop.

One story got more attention than the others.

It happened in Montana when a rare Democrat sheriff cooperated with a SAFE request sent out to all law enforcement agencies across the nation, asking the location of any known hotbeds of armed prepper or militia type activities.

This local sheriff, a man who had seen too many suicides by despondent farmers—still the most likely people in America to kill themselves with a gun—and had, years ago, been moved by the rash of school shootings and other mass murders that swept the country like a bacterial plague, did not want to see another pointless death in his town.

His clan had settled in Bull Moose in the mid-1800s and never left. He had so many relatives in a fifty-mile radius that he often wondered why there were not more birth defects. But most of his kin were, like him, good people who cared about one another, their town, their state, and their country. They did not all vote blue—those were in the minority—but they all cared deeply about the role of law in civilized society, the need for decency when dealing with one another, and the sanctity of life.

So, it came as no surprise to anyone when Sheriff Fulton Newsome alerted SAFE to what locals called "The nuts out in Grass Canyon"—or more simply, The Compound. Everyone within a hundred miles of Bull Moose knew about The Compound, about its hardcore survivalist residents and their agenda—that being to interact as little as possible with other folks and prepare for war with the United States government. Since no overt actions had taken place in the three decades since The Compound had been established and grown to a hundred or so men, women, and children—all armed, all the time—no one paid them much mind.

No one who did not live there ventured into Grass

Canyon, either.

But everyone knew, including—especially—Sheriff Newsome. He had had to serve a warrant "up in there" once and took his own small army with him. A dozen county deputies provided backup when Fulton approached the steel gate in the fifteen-foot-high concrete walls topped with broken glass, imbedded inverted nails, and rows and rows of razor wire. It made him wonder how they made enough money to pay for all this, but not enough to ask.

As it turned out, Rule Number One in The Compound was that "EVERYONE WORKS!" It was posted and preached everywhere inside. Fulton Newsome could see it from the gate when a guard opened it wide as if challenging Newsome and his deputies to just try and come through.

Sheriff Fulton Newsome was a congenial fellow, however. He got along with most everyone who was not too drunk to recognize the humanity in him. The Compound guard facing Newsome did not see it, but it didn't matter. Fulton said, "Not here to cause anyone no trouble. But there's a feller here, name of Jonathan Welker, who's wanted by the FBI for a double homicide down near Browning, in Missouruh. Now, I know this Welker fella is new here. He's not one of your old timers or other longtime residents. So, you don't owe him nothin'. And if you let him stay, out of some dumb reason of loyalty that I doubt he has for you…." Newsome paused, then said, "He didn't mention the double homicide when he asked to set up camp here, I'm guessing."

The guard remained steely-eyed and silent, but Fulton could tell he heard what was being said in between the actual words.

"Anyway," Newsome said, "I'm also guessin' ya'll don't really want to mix it up with the Bureau over harboring a known fugitive—especially one kil't a woman and her daughter after raping them. Report said he went on to rape 'em some more—*after* he killed 'em, you see.

"I'm sure you're gettin' the ugly picture loud and clear. So, as a courtesy, when I saw it come over the wire, I determined to take my chances and come on out ahead of those Bureau boys—well, they got women now too, I suppose, even in the field. But they're all pretty well-trained, I suppose, so it don't matter. They'll get their man one way or the other. I'm just tryin' to save you folks a fire fight you don't need. He ain't one'a your'n, this Welker. So I'm also guessin' it ain't worth the aggravation to you."

The beard-heavy guard never flinched, never gave an inkling as to what he might be thinking; but Fulton knew. He finished with, "So, if you'd be kind enough to run this by Helman, I'd appreciate it. I'll wait here."

And he turned around.

A moment later, he heard the gate close and felt relief—that and seeing those other twelve men with hands on the butts of their weapons. He told his deputies, "Don't reckon we'll be needin' those."

They heard him and understood, but no one moved a hand.

The reason Fulton felt confident that he would have Jonathan Welker in custody within five minutes was that he had broken a golden rule at The Compound and mentioned their leader by name. Helman—two syllables that were certain to make people cross to the other side of the street. Though no one knew for sure that he had killed anyone in cold blood—or a hundred more with his bare hands or a fucking spoon—rumors abounded. Like the one about never saying his name, maintaining his anonymity, and never bringing attention to the cult's leader lest he might have to take on the world—and win, most likely. Or die trying, along with anyone else in range.

Bull Moose was not exactly a metropolis.

Less than three minutes later, the sheriff and his posse heard a scuffle inside, close to the wall—lots of shouting, some punches, some pain—and the gate opened. Someone—several someones—threw Jonathan Welker out at Newsome's feet. Before the wanted murderer could try to flee, Newsome had a heavy, thick-calved foot on his throat and calmly said to his deputies, "Boys." Four of them came over, cuffed Welker, and dragged him to a sheriff's Explorer with a cage behind the driver's seat, chaining him to the floor in the back. He spit flames with his eyes but never said a word.

Sheriff Newsome was relieved that it went so well and turned to thank whoever might still be standing in the open gate. The only one there was the same guard from before, and he still did not speak—but someone did. A voice came from the shadows to say, "Don't ever be here again."

Newsome could not see, but he knew it was Helman.

Sheriff Fulton Newsome left with his posse and did not return. He did, however, remember what he had seen and what he had heard and what he knew to be fact, even if it was just a hunch. And when he filled out that confidential, encrypted online questionnaire and sent it back, he included a map.

Three days later, a full SAFE team arrived, consulted briefly with Sheriff Newsome, then waited for more backup. Two days after that, they cautiously approached The Compound gate.

The hundred or so SAFE agents and their backup team did not even get close before the Never Enders opened fire with what sounded like everything they had—four .50 caliber military mounted machine guns, rocket-powered grenades, mortars, and countless full-auto military-grade assault rifles.

They were not messing around.

The SAFE team retreated and called in a U.S. Air Force drone armed with a camera and several missiles. When Helman ordered the drone shot down, the SAFE crew watched on a monitor as he pointed up, and his people scrambled to bring out a surface to air missile launcher, or Stinger.

Carter Smith also watched back in D.C. "Holy shit," he said. "These clowns are serious."

"As a heart attack," someone added, because that was what he always said.

"Do we have a plane up?" Smith asked.

"Yes, sir. Locked and loaded," the same underling said. He liked to sound like the cliché of power he thought himself to be.

Before any further orders could be given from Washington, the field SAFE officers launched the drone's missiles, which proved deadly accurate, taking out the structure they locked on. This caused more scampering down below—compounders running for just-uncovered entrances to a bunker below, pouring in like ants as the Stinger man launched. The blast caused him to fall over backwards, but two seconds later, the drone image went to static as the little beast exploded and its remnants fell to the ground in flames.

Someone on a radio said, "Them's fightin' words," and the next thing to come over the encrypted airwaves was, "Hitman, are you in position?"

The pilot of the Air National Guard F-22 said, "Roger. Permission to engage."

Carter Smith nodded to his head of aviation tacticals—

the head of the Air Force — who said into his mic, "Permission to engage affirmed. Take 'em out," with as little emotion as ordering a cheese Danish.

Though not all the folks at The Compound had made it all the way to their steel-reinforced cement deep-underground bunker, they made sure that Helman had, as most of the others filtered down, ready — or so they thought.

Up above, Hitman touched his launch buttons, and two spent uranium-tipped Bunker Busters sped for "home."

Had anyone been able to peer through the ground and concrete, they would have seen a remarkable feat of warfare engineering as the two missiles cut through it all like a warm knife through warm oleo — directly into the bunker, where they exploded precisely as commanded.

On the surface, there was a dull *whump,* and the ground rose in a swell, then dropped several feet below what it had been, like an instant sinkhole. To say nothing was left down below was to ignore the existence of unbridled fire, evaporated weaponry — not even including the secondaries — and burning tidbits of bone and flesh.

The Compound was no more — at least as a place, a thing.

But it made news. One problem had been solved, but many more created. Every channel had a slant on the attack — from "This was to be expected" to questions about the possible use of "excessive force," to "A full-blown attack on our freedoms!" and variations on a violation of the Constitution regarding "using our military for a police action."

The sources for each easily imagined.

On his newly reminted mid-afternoon show, Brian Williams had the lede. "There is a new concern that the federal government may be going too far in its effort to enforce the newly enacted GCA law. This report from Genna Lowry outside Bull Moose, Montana."

Genna Lowry was a light-skinned African-Asian-American woman too young, too pretty, and too delicate to be a field reporter, but there she was. What she lacked in experience, she made up for in grit and tenacity.

Bravery.

Wearing a flak jacket the network required, she walked up to anyone she could find on the mostly deserted streets of Bull Moose. No one in those parts wanted to be national news. They were already embarrassed that their town was all over cable.

Sheriff Fulton Newsome refused all interviews, referring reporters to SAFE, and hid in the back room of his jailhouse. Deputies had instructions to keep all the doors locked and talk to no one. The phones were ringing off the hooks.

Out on Main Street, Genna Lowry found one man willing to talk. He said his name was George but declined to give a last name—while on camera, in full view, in front of his store, on Main Street in Bull Moose, Montana.

The banner said so.

George was mad as hell. He would be bleeped in the innumerable rebroadcasts, but for now, they had to let it stand. "The gov'ment's gone too damn far! Those were peaceful people minding their own goddamn business out there. Gov'ment had no right killing 'em all like that. Women and children."

Genna said, "But isn't it true they had stockpiled weapons of mass destruction?"

"Oh hell, woman, they didn't have anything like that. I never seen it."

Over at the jail, one of the deputies came into the back room to tell his sheriff that, "George Toddy's on the TV."

"Oh hell," Fulton said, shaking his head. He knew exactly what George would say—and why. The Compound folks were his main customers. He had made a living for twenty years on their business alone. Now that was gone for good.

Fulton sighed and said, "Turn it on," with as much enthusiasm as telling his dentist, Dr. Gene Krohn, to "go ahead and pull it."

Genna Lowry was saying, "Initial government reports from the site detail weapons parts from literally thousands of assault rifles, dozens of rocket-propelled launchers, and several surface to air missiles—most of them of Russian or Chinese origin—and perhaps millions of rounds of ammunition." She looked at her phone and read, "The partial list, just so far, says 'the government has confirmed evidence of the existence of AR-15s, M-16s, Kalashnikovs, Tech 9s and 11s, Type 91s, Type 93s, Type 95s—those are Chinese assault rifles—dozens of crates of hand grenades, rocket-propelled grenades, and two other Stinger missile launchers with full armament.'"

She looked at George, who really got riled up. "That's a buncha horseshit! I never saw any'a that crap!"

Fulton, watching his TV, said, "Because you never went out there, George. But don't mention that part." His sarcasm was sharp enough to elicit chuckles from his men. They all knew George Tolly and his sympathies—for anyone with cash.

Most locals referred to "George's Folly."

Tolly told Lowry, "I got nothin' else to say except this administration has gone asswipe batshit, killin' decent Americans whose only fault is arming themselves to protect themselves against the goddamned tyrannical government that's out to git 'em. And look what happened! Goddamn government ambushed 'em while they was eatin' breakfast and nuked 'em with a goddamned bunker buster. Killed ever' last goddamn one of 'em. I got nothin' else to say."

One of Newsome's deputies editorialized, "That's even more than he usually doesn't say," getting a chuckle from his boss, who knew to laugh now while he still could because this was not going away anytime soon.

Lowry pressed her interviewee. "But didn't their leader Harold Helman send a letter to the White House, daring them to come and try to take his weapons? Didn't he also make a video of himself shooting at a passing police car?"

"Shit, that was years ago," George said, waving it off. "And so what? We all do and say shit we don't mean. He was scared like we all are! All we want is to keep our guns for protection like the Second Amendment guarantees us, so we can defend ourselves against our government if we have to—like *now*." He was brimming with rancidifying self-righteousness.

"Ol' George is on a roll," a deputy said.

"He knows he'll have to go back to depending on the rest of us to keep him afloat," another said.

And Fulton Newsome, kind man that he was, said, "We'll do what we can."

No one else had another comment.

Genna Lowry, even more bravely, told George, "That amendment was deemed 'outdated and irrelevant' by the Supreme Court of the United States—six to three, surprisingly."

"Well fuck them and their horse, too," George said. "I got nothin' else to say except whoever heard of the Supreme Court goin' against the Constitution of the United States? For shit's sake! I never heard of such a thing. Decent people being slaughtered wholesale in the streets by the thousands." He had digressed, careened off his intended path of common-sense persuasion to anxious hyperbole.

Genna eyed him rubbing the heel of his Frontier revolver but said, "I believe that actual number is less than ten, nationally—only those who resisted or opened fire first."

"Shitfire, woman! There was two-three hundred of 'em just out there!" He pointed. "Maybe a thousand or more!" He huffed and said, "Ten my ass. And I'm supposed to believe *you*? Goddamn fake mainstream media. I'm s'posed to be impressed by *that*? Killin's killin'. I got nothin' else to say. America's been killin'-in-the-name-of since we was born a country. Ain't gonna stop now just because they think they can take everyone's goddamn guns away."

Feeling empowered, Genna said to George, "Speaking of that, how is it that you still have *your* gun, George? We're live around the world, right now."

George looked down. His eyes went wide, and he hurried back inside his store.

In the back of the jailhouse, laughter peeled.

Genna Lowry, feeling damn good about what was only her third field interview, turned back to the camera and said only, "Brian."

In studio, Williams said, "We'll have more as this story develops, of course. Coming up, the gun ban hits a hundred—a hundred million, that is. Stay with us."

The camera cut to a shot from the demolished compound, a zoom-in on a handmade poster with charred edges. The words read "Death to Federal Fascism!" The image showed jackboots trampling the American flag.

"And…we're out," someone said.

Brian Williams spun his chair around to face his producer.

He said, "They had Stingers, really? And we deployed an F-22 with bunker busters? What the hell is going on?"

Even Brian Williams was at a loss for further words.

CHAPTER TWELVE

D.C. looked like a warzone as if a coup happened, and now the government had hardened the targets. Jets and helicopters flew overhead in a crisscross pattern every few minutes, covering the grid with certainty. Warships sailed the Potomac. Half the army seemed to be stationed at the White House, with the other half at the Capitol. If a real war started anywhere in the world, whoever got sent over might well feel alone — not to mention safer.

Otherwise, the town felt deserted. Tourism had been suspended. Automobile traffic was halted. Only buses and necessary delivery trucks were allowed on the streets. And all of them, buses and trucks, were subject to random stops and searches.

Maybe not so random.

All public buildings were closed to the public, and only employees were allowed in — after a thorough TSA-style X-ray, wand, and body search. No one was taking any chances. One nut with a gun could do a lot of damage to the program, the person, and the president, whose poll ratings were already in the tank, the lowest of any president ever — and less than a week in.

Pinkins did not mind. Keeping his eye on "the end of

this thing," which was inevitable — eventually, though no one could guess when — he did his best to keep the rest of the government functioning while GCA ran its course. He knew the process would take time, and even when it was over, it would not really be over, possibly for years.

Hopefully in his lifetime.

A few blocks away, a decaying federal edifice was surrounded by scaffolding, getting a thorough retrofit. Signs informed anyone interested that the building was under repair "indefinitely." No projected end date. The Not Presently Open to the Public signs meant little to anyone passing since no other buildings in Metro center were open to the public, either.

Nobody could remember what the building had been, what agency had been in it, or when it had closed — how long ago — but it was dead outside. No workers, no traffic in or out, no signs of life. However....

Deep underground, in a secret level even deeper than the high-security basement offices, business was booming. There were no windows so far underground, so day/night issues had no grip. The hidden floor operated 24/7 without interruption. Hundreds of handpicked men and women in camo — no Kevlar vests, as they were in no way concerned about a breach — moved about purposefully, without haste, doing...whatever it was they were doing.

A large sign read, NO Weapons on Site — This Means YOU!

In the main command and control center sat a single, large desk. Behind that desk were two placards — seals of an organization or its central tenet. This was not the CIA, nor the FBI, nor ATF, nor any other known government entity.

The first large round seal sported raised images of two

AR-15s crossed under a skull. Nested below the imagery were the words, *Ad Finem*…To the End. The other seal featured a map of America made of handguns woven into Old Glory. It read, *Ad Victorem Ire Spolia.* To the victor go the spoils.

A large man of average height with a full head of thick grey hair — muscular, overly healthy for his mid-fifties; a former U.S. Marine captain turned financier — sat at the desk, smoking a fat cigar, tapping it occasionally on a placard that read No Smoking to drop his ash in a crystal bowl on the other side. As with everyone else in this federal dungeon, he wore no name tag, though it was clear that he was The Man in Charge. Everyone allowed into his office knew who he was — Harris Ball.

Everyone also knew his never-spoken-aloud nickname.

Ball was reading an article in *The Wall Street Journal* headlined "Market Hits New Low on Gun Law Losses." He grunted and turned the page as a young Asian-American man named Mike Cho came in. A U.S. Army sergeant on active reserve duty, Cho was also of average height, but slender, if extremely fit.

He was also fidgety. "You asked to see me, sir?"

"Sit down, Mike," Harris Ball told him and put down his *WSJ*, but not his cigar. "What's the latest from the hinterlands?"

Cho said, "Everything seems to be progressing smoothly."

"No new wholesale slaughter of women and children?"

"Not since the Montana thing. SAFE has been more careful."

"I'd say," Harris said without irony.

Cho reported, "Minor skirmishes, a few arrests for concealment or resisting, but other than that, most civilians seem to be complying with the law without incident. Polls show strong approval. I heard there was a parade in Illinois somewhere. Two-hundred thousand people marched in support of the president and GCA."

"Hmm," Ball said. "Hadn't heard that."

"It was a lot of people, sir."

Ball leaned forward. "Are you implying that I should read more, Cho?" His words were pointed, but he had a dance in his eye.

"No, sir," Cho said. "I'm sure you have enough to do."

"Shit!" Ball said, leaning back and puffing. "Down here in this hellhole? Waiting for hell to arrive? I've been busier shitting while constipated."

"Yessir, it does get kind of dull down here at times."

"That will change," Ball said, sitting up.

"I'm sure it will, sir."

"And quit calling me sir in every goddamned sentence. It's annoying as hell."

"Yessir," Cho said—his turn with the dancing eyes.

"Fuck off," Ball said.

Cho chuckled and said, "How long do you think we'll be down here?"

"Wife getting horny?"

"As an alley cat in heat."

Ball was surprised. "You don't get to go home nights?"

"Not nights or days, sir."

Ball shook his head, showing some anger. "This fucking thing."

"Yes sir," Cho agreed.

Ball dug in his desk and found a pad with pre-printed forms. He scribbled something on it, signed, then handed it to Cho. "Here. Sixteen on, eight off. Starting when we're done here."

"Thank you, sir," Cho said.

"Will you please stop that?" Ball said, getting more annoyed. "Seriously."

"Yes—," Cho said, and caught himself. "Okay," he said. "Military habit."

"Yeah, yeah," Ball said. "Military."

His tone lay somewhere between dreamy and dyspeptic. He moved a few things on his desk, just because, then said, "Well, Mr. Cho, I don't think this whole deal is gonna last much longer. I'd say we'll see action sooner than we think."

"I hope so—" He caught himself again.

Ball looked up with a furrowed but determined brow and said, "Hope is not an option, son. Fate is not a reality, and faith is never necessary. Truth is always and only enough."

Mike Cho raised his eyebrows. He had not expected philosophy. He said, "Wise words, sir. Sorry. But…you're right. That's why you're where you are today, and I'm over here."

Bothered by the sycophantic sounds of that, Ball told Cho to, "Get outa here."

Cho tamed his cultured response of a salute and chose a smile instead as he turned and walked away, Harris Ball yelling after him: "And you're *not* here. None of us are."

He heard Cho say back, "No, sir."

Chapter Thirteen

In the Surge Room at the White House, concerns had heated up, along with tempers. DNI Porter Clausen took one look at all the red blinking lights on the world map—indicators of hot spots with the potential for conflict—and exploded at the CIA's #2, a woman named Haskell—Edie Haskell.

Her nickname was even easier than Harris Ball's.

"What in the good name of HELL is going on?" Clausen screamed.

A high-ranking air force general standing nearby could barely contain himself from saying, *Yep. Looks like we're in a pickle, Porter.*

Deputy Director Haskell said, "Sources in the Middle East and Africa tell us that everyone is saying now is their time. They figure we're in a weakened state, focused on our domestic *issue* as we are. Our thinking is that we should prepare for an outside attack, which we feel is imminent."

Clausen glanced at the president and shook his head. "Christ," he said to Haskell. "From where?"

Haskell said, "We aren't sure, so we have to assume from everywhere."

"Oh, for fuck's sake," Clausen said, and turned to the president. "Mr. President, sir. Isn't there something you can do to help us?"

"And what would that be, Porter?"

"I don't know, sir. Stop this whole gun craziness."

Pinkins chuckled. "It was gun craziness that got us here to begin with."

"I understand that, sir," Clausen said. "But couldn't you at least slow it down some, relieve some of the pressure on our troops over there?"

Pinkins said, "I wish I could, Porter. Believe me. I don't want them in harm's way any more than you do. But my hands are tied. GCA was signed into law by my predecessor, and until Congress or the Supreme Court finds a way to undo it or figures out a way to put a temporary halt to it, there is nothing I or you or anyone else can do. The law stipulates that we are to move as swiftly as is possible to ameliorate the possibility of backsliding."

"You could pretend to be moving full throttle, sir, but...."

Pinkins gave Clauson a moment to complete his thought. When he did not, Pinkins said, "You can always take it up with your legislator. I hear that Congresswoman Maxwell is still shifting uncomfortably on that fence rail. Maybe she has a way to lie to the American public that hasn't occurred to the rest of us."

Porter looked like he needed a TUMs. Maybe a whole bottle.

President Pinkins patted him on the shoulder and said again, "I understand your concerns, and I share them. But I ask that you be patient. Sally and I are working on this thing from our end the best we can. We have many friends on both sides of the aisle, waiting to jump. But they need a bigger reason than a minority of Americans not liking the law. In the meantime, the faster we get it over with, the better off we'll be."

"If the country doesn't blow itself up or we get pulled into an uncontrollable conflict over there — maybe *everywhere* over there," Clausen said dourly, getting nods from his military equals.

"Well," Pinkins said diplomatically, "let's keep our fingers crossed. Sally?" He turned to his VP, then walked out. She gave a last raised eyebrow to the worried room then followed.

In the Oval Office, Pinkins was pacing when Hawkins entered. He asked her, "What are we going to do, Sal?"

His vice president said, "We could start bringing troops home to help here. That would kill two birds with one shot, if I may mix my metaphor in a dark way."

Pinkins almost chuckled but pointed out, "You know we can't do that."

"Mix our metaphors?" she said.

"That too," he said.

Sally Hawkins understood that he meant to use the U.S. military to act as national police — even pretending to. She said, "I was thinking military bases and port cities, airports, international entry points."

Pinkins ran it through his internal processor a moment, then said, "We might get away with that. But what good would it do? How many guns would we find? We have some 250 million to go, by the lowest estimate. Nabbing a few dopes at the airport stupid enough to carry in a weapon won't do much to help our cause."

"Not that it is our cause," she said.

"It is until it isn't," Pinkins said, then sat behind the Resolute desk.

Hawkins sat across from him and said, "One thing's for

sure: we're going to have to bump up the Security Council meeting. I've never seen that many red zones on the Big Map in my life." Sally Hawkins had been a congresswoman and a senator for two decades before accepting Pinkins' request to be his VP.

The president shook his head, feeling fatigue creeping in. Already. "You're my foreign affairs veteran," he said. "What do you really think is going on? What *will* happen as opposed to what might happen."

Hawkins said, "I think it's entirely possible that we are going to see attacks on our bases abroad. I don't think there's any question about that. We've got our heads so far up our own asses on this GCA thing, we couldn't handle more than a minor incident or two outside the country, and they know that. I think they are going to take advantage of it. Where? I can't tell you, and neither can the IC, either. At least at this early point. We might just have to wait and see what flares up first. Then we'll know."

"That's not what I wanted to hear."

"We don't hear much of what we want to hear these days."

"Ain't that the truth," Pinkins said, shaking his head.

Sally Hawkins tried her original idea again. "Look, all I'm saying is that if we brought some troops home, it would show our enemies that we're not concerned about their actions overseas. That our priority *is* here at home."

"Would that not encourage them to attack?"

"Maybe—but maybe not. It could be a solid feint. They would be caught off guard by our reducing troop strengths in their areas. They would have to wonder why. And we don't have to give numbers. Maybe put up a few extra sorties for show here and there. They would likely come to the conclusion—even if it's wrong—that we are so prepared we aren't worried. That we'll rain 'fire and fury' down on them if they try anything. That we aren't even going to bother with boots on the ground. So they might, in the end, be more cautious—and reluctant. In the meantime, we get extra help with GCA."

"Ohhh," Pinkins sighed. "You had me at *The Art of War* counter-intuitive reverse-logic bit. But we cannot in any way use American troops to patrol or police or even ride around while armed, and you know it."

"We could if we can get Congress to invoke the Insurrection Act to override Posse Comitatus."

As Pinkins paused to consider this route, Sally raised her eyebrows again, as she was wont to do more than the president liked. He said, "You think they would?"

Sally was blunt. "If someone declares war on us."

"Ha!" Pinkins said. "We should be so lucky."

As it turned out, luck was lurking 1,500 miles southwest — in Austin.

***

At the Texas Statehouse, a wiry Republican in a white ten-gallon hat and ostrich boots stood in the chamber and said, "Mr. Speaker, if I may, I would like to suggest Bill 4739a, and move that the great state of Texas secede from the Union of the States." One of his fellow zealots seconded the motion to rumbles of approval mixed with shock.

Not that anyone should have been shocked.

The speaker said, "You mean to secede from the United States of America, sir?"

"I do, Mr. Speaker," the first lunatic said. "I do indeed. I further request an immediate up or down vote. Hell, I *demand* it!"

Cheers roared through the halls as 850 miles to the northeast in the Tennessee House, a similar bill had just been introduced and was getting a similar up or down vote. No one was surprised that the loud "Ayes" overpowered the weak "Nays" by sixty decibels, and Tennessee officially seceded from the union.

At least on paper.

Though a few other states—the usual suspects—considered similar secession motions, none made it to a vote. For the time being, the Republic of Texas, and the more plainly named Tennessee, were on their own.

Roger Pinkins could not have been happier. Close to forty-million now former Americans did not have to be searched and forced to turn over their one-hundred million guns. The schedule had bumped itself up without him raising a finger—or the risky Comitatus question.

POTUS's full cabinet assembled in less than an hour for an emergency meeting regarding the double secession. Pinkins asked to dispose of formality and "Cut to the chase."

Sally Hawkins took the reins. "Gentlemen, ladies," she started formally. "As you now are no doubt aware, Texas and Tennessee have announced that they will secede from the United States."

The secretary of the treasury—who had already done some quick math in his head on the way over, with the help of four aides using phone calculators—said, "And?" The Texas economy ranked second in the U.S. That might be a problem. But Tennessee, at eighteenth—not so much.

Sally Hawkins said, "And…we agreed. Or as I said to Governors Alamo and Beauregard, 'Good riddance, boys.'" She knew those were not their names but had never liked either one of them. Chuckles erupted, and a smattering of concerned groans. Hawkins went on. "Following on that note, since the two states are no longer states, but are de facto countries no longer associated with the United States of America, and since they have both stated hostile intents, based on their decisions not to implement GCA—"

"If I may jump in," Attorney General Lanciter said.

Sally Hawkins said, "Please."

Lanciter said, "The states' attorneys general have both filed petitions stating that if any agents of the federal government set foot on their soil, with or without the intention of disarming their citizens, they will take it as an act of war and respond accordingly."

Laughs went around the room.

Sally added, "Both states have deployed National Guard troops to defend their borders. Tennessee is talking about building a wall and making North Carolina, Virginia, Kentucky, Missouri, Arkansas, Mississippi, Alabama, and Georgia pay for it."

This brought the biggest guffaws yet.

However, AG Lanciter killed the bit when he said, "At least one federal agent has been murdered in each state of Texas and Tennessee."

Laughter halted.

VP Hawkins said, "We can only view these treacheries as acts of war." She let that settle in the room like someone else's fart in a hot shower.

The head of the Commerce Department, a youngish Hispanic-American woman from Laredo, said, "Um...what does that mean, exactly?"

"It means," Sally Hawkins, Vice President of the United States, said, "We are at war."

The Laredo woman paled—her entire family lived in

Laredo — and she said, "With Texas?"

"And Tennessee," Pinkins threw in.

"Holy shit," Enriqua Cortez-Hightower said — and ran from the room to call home.

She was followed out by most of the rest of the cabinet, especially the head of Housing and Urban Welfare, a chubby ex-preacher from Knoxville, all of them frantically speed-dialing.

Pinkins turned to his defense secretary, Rear Admiral Geneva Hampton-Byers, and said, "Madam Secretary, bring our troops home."

She said, "All of them, sir?"

"No, just ten or twenty thousand," he said. "Wherever they're not essential to our mission."

"Which mission is that, sir?"

"Maintaining our position as a global imperialistic power."

"Sir?"

Sally Hawkins said, "If they ain't fightin', they're flightin'." She grinned.

The order went out.

Around the globe, happy service men and women packed up their gear and headed for the tarmac. There were so many troop transport planes in the air at once, ground control *lost* control at one point. But everyone would get home safely.

Failsafe planes were sent aloft again, and every submarine in the fleet dove into deeper waters, then shifted to more strategic locales within range of possible flare-up regions and targets. Satellites went abuzz with new life and orbits. The United States had officially gone rogue — on itself.

The world noticed.

CHAPTER FOURTEEN

President Roger Pinkins heard the door of the Oval Office open and looked up to see his vice president Sally Hawkins approaching to ask him, "Did you see Omaha?"

"Bunch of angry screaming white folks?"

"That'd be them."

"Has Nebraska seceded yet?"

"Not yet. But nine other states are considering bills, and fifteen more have threatened to consider bills."

"State politics in action."

"Inaction," she said.

"I have to say, I did not see that one coming."

"No one said this job would be easy."

"Well, one did," Pinkins said. "And look what happened to him."

"Proves there's karma, I suppose."

"If nothing else."

"Did you see the Taco Loco thing?" Sally said. Pinkins shook his head. "Oh, *well*," his VP said, and sat. "Let me tell you." Her story started earlier that late morning.

***

A twenty-year-old white kid named Chuck pulled into his local Taco Loco outside Tampa during the noon rush.

At the drive-up speaker, a bored teenage girl's voice said in monotone, "Welcome to Taco Loco. How can I make you crazy happy today?"

Chuck said he could think of a few ways.

Having heard every dumbass line in existence, a thousand times each, the girl said, "May I take your order, sir?"

Chuck said, "Yes, you may, ma'am. I'd like two Taco Locos and an Insane Burrito with Crazy Cheese and extra Loco Sauce, and an extra-large Loco-Cola."

Nine seconds later, the girl said, "That'll be nine-seventy-three. Pull up to the second window to get your mentally ill order."

She was just supposed to say, "your totally mental order," but it was only eleven-fifteen, and she had already had a shitty day, so why not inject a little of her personalized humor.

By the time Chuck paid and accepted a receipt, his order was up and in a bag. The same teen, a post-Goth girl with posts and the tattoo of a pirate rat on each ear, handed out the wildly colored red and yellow and black paper bag with a cartoon Mexican bandito strapped with quadruple bandoliers, big white teeth that sparkled, and a completely deranged mien under the logo "Insanely good!"

She repeated his order as she had been trained to do. "That's two Taco Locos, an Insane Burrito with Crazy Cheese and extra Loco Sauce, and an extra-large Loca-Cola."

"You got it," Chuck said amiably, and took the bag.

She said, as flatly as was possible, "Have a crazy day," and closed the window.

"I think I will," Chuck said, placing the bag on his passenger seat and retrieving his father's Kel-Tec PMR-30—the latter figure being the number of rounds in its magazine—and opened fire through the window, shattering the glass, peppering the inside of the order bay, and killing her.

Charles David Goren then drove to the Wait Here for Special Orders space, parked, and got out of his Blazer, taking a hundred-round AR15 with full-auto modifications — fully illegal even before GCA — and a similarly modified TEC-9 he bought on the street before The Purge, as his father called the new law. It held only thirty-two rounds but could be emptied before anyone realized there was a danger. "Zero to 32 in under three seconds," his father always said when praising his son's buyer awareness and "purchasing power."

Inside the fast-food restaurant, customers were unsure what had happened, looking back to see what all the employee screaming was about. No one noticed when Chuck stepped in front of the large plate glass window, a weapon in each hand, and let fly. He did not even bother going in. In less than fifteen seconds, he had killed nine people and wounded another seven.

He said, "Take that motherfuckers." Only he knew he was talking to the president and the federal government in general.

He then climbed back in his Blazer and pulled away, already digging into his lunch bag with keen interest. He found the first Taco Loco and took a bite. "Crazy good," he said. And drove for his next soft target.

***

Roger Pinkins asked Sally Hawkins, "Did he get away?"

"That time," she said.

"Jesus," Pinkins said.

His VP said, "Not only that, two customers inside the store were armed and shot each other."

Pinkins' eyes narrowed. He said, "See, this is why —" and stopped himself. They both knew why. He asked, "Did they…were they confused?"

"No," she said. "Just apparently bad shots."

"Aiming for the kid."

"So they said."

"Unbelievable."

"It gets better." By better, she meant worse — much worse.

***

While Tampa police and Hillsborough County sheriffs searched for the white or tan or yellow or black or red or blue Blazer — no one from the Taco Loco could agree on its color — Chuck parked across the street from the Happy Gaspar Assisted Living Facility with its "gay" pirate on the sign (built in the 1960s, remodeled but never renamed or logo'd), and bit into his Insane Burrito, again saying, "Crazy good," because he always did because he liked saying it.

And he watched.

Because the nursing home had a wall of windows in the front, he could see most of what was going on inside the large main lobby to make up his mind on how, or if, to proceed. He already had a plan; he just needed to make sure it was viable.

What he could not see was that inside the Happy Gaspar Assisted Living Facility, several of the seniors were veterans and were packing. And they were *very* determined not to give up their guns. Though the staff was aware of the problem, there was little they could do, as every time they approached an armed old guy requesting the weapon, they received a death threat.

They came up with a solution to solve their little dilemma and not look bad to the residents while doing it. They made a phone call to the 1-800-SAFE-NOW line to let the somewhat surprised volunteer operator know that the Happy Gaspar Assisted Living Facility was more of a WWII machine-gun nest of cranky old people.

Some with dementia.

SAFE's response coincided with young Chuck's surveillance. So, even though he was unaware that he would have been met with multiple angles of rapid fire that would have been far more accurate than the loaded bozos at the Taco Loco, he did scrunch down in his seat when he saw the SAFE vehicles arrive with the usual local backup in case of arrests—though what warrants the cops expected to serve in the nursing home was never clear.

Peering over his windowsill, waiting for the cops to be focused in the other direction, Chuck watched as, inside the Happy Gaspar, all hell broke loose. He could not hear what was being said, but if he could have, it would have gone something like:

"It's the heat!"

"They're onto us!"

"Run!"

Which was more roll.

Chuck could just see a large screen TV set playing live footage from the Taco Loco he had ambushed, where ambulances and police and reporters now swarmed the place. He wished he could see the body count, but he was too far away to read the banner.

And there was the potted palm.

As the SAFE agents entered the lobby en masse, Chuck discreetly pulled away for his next possible soft-target attack site.

***

"How do we know all this?" Pinkins asked his VP.

"Local cops put it together in hindsight."

Pinkins understood. "They realized the car was his but

didn't notice until too late."

Hawkins nodded. "They were busy recovering 137 guns from the old folks and twelve from the staff."

Pinkins shook his head. "What are these people thinking?"

"That they love their guns and don't want us taking them."

Pinkins shook his head again and said, "Well, at least they were onto the kid."

"Not so fast," Sally said.

***

After finishing his Insane Burrito, his other Loco Taco, and most of his extra-large Loco-Cola, Chuck—who always errantly called it a Loca-Cola because it sounded better to him, more mellifluous, less crazy—nodded to himself. He had entered the address of his next possible mass-murder site, and the nice iPhone lady led him straight to the front door of the Macy G. Dawes Children's Cancer Clinic.

This time, Chuck took both fully-loaded hundred-round ARs, cinched up his Kevlar vest, stepped out of his Blazer, took a last hit of *Loca*-Cola, and threw the cup to the ground like a contentedly angry Clint Eastwood about to mow down the last of the bad guys. Only this time, in Chuck's movie, the vengeance-motif had more to do with getting even with those meddling government motherfuckers, by going after the most publicity-creating innocent victims he could find: kids with cancer.

His father would be proud.

With a smile on his face and a burning desire in his heart to be heartless— "for the cause"—Chuck strode for the main entry of the large hospital. He had reloaded the TEC-9 and stuffed it into his belt, along with the Kel-Tec PMR and a plain old 15-round Glock 19, his cargo-pants pockets filled with as many extra clips as he could stuff into them.

There would be no one in a kids' cancer hospital to stop him, so he had visions of dancing, plum-eating happy bears in his mind as the double doors glided open and he stepped inside.

***

President Roger Pinkins hung his head. "Oh, Jesus," he said.

"Just wait," Sally Hawkins said — and POTUS wondered why she was smiling.

She was smiling because the moment Chuck set foot in the lobby of the Macy G. Dawes Children's Cancer Clinic and yelled, "For the children!" just inside the second set of silent sliding glass doors, the black security guard — a young guy named DeJan, just twenty-four — who had seen him coming, stepped in from Chuck's blindside, from behind a thick column, and put one through Chuck's crazy-loco head. Chuckie dropped like a sack of wet cement, blood shooting ten feet from his opposite temple.

"Thank God!" Pinkins said.

"I know, right?" Sally Hawkins said. "But get this."

"Oh Jesus, what?"

"Police charged the guard with possessing an illegal handgun."

"Get the fuck out."

"Arrested him, threw him in lockup, bail. Because of the 'murder,' they said."

Pinkins' head swung around as the thoughts inside it no doubt were making him swirl. "Is there something we can do?"

"Not unless we want to get called out for ignoring our own law that we are bound and determined to enforce."

"Bastards," was all Pinkins could come up with on such short notice. He did not need to be specific.

Sally said, "Good news is the mayor of Tampa has promised the kid—"

"The guard?"

"The guard, yes, an award—the Morris Pantucket Medal of Personal Valor or something—and the key to the city. Providing he gets out of jail before the world ends."

"What have we created?" Pinkins said to no one.

"I think you know the answer to that," Sally Hawkins said as she stood then exited.

Pinkins knew well. It may not have been his creation, but it was his baby now.

CHAPTER FIFTEEN

Pinkins' chief of staff, Roald Dullea, had been summoned to the Oval Office for an update. Keeping up on everything had become impossible with a single daily briefing. Pinkins asked, "Anyone offer to surrender yet?"

"Not yet," Dullea said. "But a group of 'concerned citizens' from Tennessee has gathered four-hundred-thousand signatures for a petition to rejoin the union, and we received a petition signed by six-hundred-thousand 'concerned citizens of Texas' requesting an embassy to negotiate a surrender of the United States of America to the Great Republic of Texas. Russia and Venezuela have offered humanitarian support to both states in 'their struggle against imperialist oppression,' and Mexico has offered to take back Texas if it's on the market. But they said we can keep the panhandle. They don't want it."

"Tell them all or nothing," Pinkins said.

"At least they're providing a nice distraction."

The president could not argue with that tenet. He asked about Congress. "Are they doing anything over there? Anything at all?"

"A bill has reached the floor for vote called the Honesty and Integrity in Campaign Contribution and Underlying Programs."

"HICCUP?"

"Uh-huh."

Pinkins shook his head, fully aware that he was doing that a lot, and asked, "What's it say?"

"If a candidate for office knowingly lies about their opponent during a campaign, he or she is banned from running for office for ten years. If a subordinate lies and the candidate knew about it, then it's only five years. They think they have the votes."

"Who put it up?"

"House whip Cloyner."

"Tell them I'll veto."

"Will do."

"Anything else?"

"Kitchen ran out of turkey burgers, and the Turkey Farmers' Union has declined to provide more unless they are given a waiver to keep their guns."

"To execute the turkeys?"

"No, probably their aim is more in your direction."

"Ah. Well then, tell them no. We'll stick with chicken."

"There's more of it."

"My thinking."

Pinkins stood and turned to look out into the Rose Garden, where at least a hundred armed troops stood stationed at the ready. "Do you think we can trust them?" he said.

"Hard to say."

"Mmm."

Pinkins turned back. "How are we doing on the National Guard and Reserve evacuations?"

"Tennessee is mostly clear. The governor realized it wasn't worth risking military lives to make a statement."

"I'd say he already made his statement."

"And they're landlocked."

"Mexico won't be invading them anytime soon. Have they asked for international aid?"

"Not yet."

"Texas?"

"The governor tweeted that any foreign military personnel—"

"Wait. He did not mean—"

"Yes, he did," Dullea said with a glimmer. "I believe his exact words were 'United States treasoners' setting foot on sovereign Texas soil would be executed."

Pinkins sat at his desk and dropped his head into his hands. "What is in the water down there?"

"Formaldehyde, I'd guess."

"What has JCoS come up with? Anything?"

"Yeah," Dullea said. "Since Governor Clupner specifically said 'setting foot,' he left room—no doubt intentionally—for air, rail, and bus evacuations."

"Ah," Pinkins said, nodding.

"We're about halfway there with the Reserves," Dullea said. "Obviously, Lackland and Fort Hood are going to take longer. And Clupner is making a States' Rights move to keep the Guard under his control."

"Have we considered just bombing the capitol in Austin?"

"It came up," Dullea said, dryly.

"And?" Dullea looked to see if his boss was serious. He was not. "Too nice'a building," he said. "Be a shame to lose such a grand structure."

"Something like that," Dullea said, appreciating the joke. "Maybe if they have a convention or something—in a Ramada."

"Works for me," Pinkins said. "Anything else?"

"Oh yeah," Dullea said. "But I think that's enough for now. I'll come back after lunch with the rest."

"Thanks. Just what my digestion needs."

"You're still digesting food? I'm impressed," Dullea said, heading for the hidden door. "Enjoy your chicken."

"Oh, you know I will."

So went every update, every day of the week, six-to-seven times a day. And that did not even include visits from Secretary of State Colleen Pleasance, JCoS Chairwoman Audrey Callahan, DNI's Clausen Porter, or the rest, making Pinkins wonder why he had accepted the nomination.

If he had only known.

By the end of the week, more than fifty skirmishes had broken out between active service folks and Texas cops, mostly highway patrolmen in their white cowpoke hats. The women wore brown hats and did not choose to engage with U.S. military forces. Governor Culpepper—as he had come to be known—fired over a thousand of them in one signing order. They did not protest. They were waiting, hopeful.

Most left the state immediately.

The men were, as usual, stupider—and in Texas, where everything is bigger, their stupidity shone on a grand scale. Six carloads of Texas Rangers stopped a busload of armed and prepared soldiers leaving Fort Hood, surrounding the bus with their vehicles and drawing weapons. The shootout was short but fierce.

Luckily for the almost-rogue HPs, the better-trained Green Berets—yes, they stopped a busload of Green Berets and fired on them—were better shots. They took out the vehicles, leaving the Rangers with nowhere to hide.

The TX Chippies raised a white Stetson on an assault rifle, and the bus shoved their shot-up Explorers out of the way, then drove without further incident to Fort Polk in Louisiana, the occasional phalanx of Vipers, Tomcats, and Raptors swooping low whenever other local law enforcement types got anywhere near.

Two B-52s were spotted over the Capital Building.

It turned out the "escape bus" was a test to see if anyone in Texas was dumb enough to try and stop it. Though surely someone might have answered that dumb question with the obvious dumb answer, the outcome proved both predictable and prescient.

Pointy-headed protesters lined roads with No More Buses Out! signs until they too were shot at by either A) angry Texans who *agreed*, or B) angry Texans who did not understand the protests — or the point.

Either way, Governor Cletus Culpepper ordered that there be no more attacks on military transports of any type. He saw the writing on the wall — literally, as someone painted graffiti on the capitol building that read, "The death of a single American soldier and we're coming for you, Cullie." Someone else tried to pun it with, "You will be Culper-able!"

Both were sandblasted off by the end of the day. But the spray-painted messages worked. Texas continued in glorious disarray, and Mexico decided they didn't want it back after all — not with all those Texans in it.

CHAPTER SIXTEEN

Late night comics continued to have a field day with the American political landscape, even if much of it was not funny anymore. The Texas "incident" did give them plenty of fodder, though.

"So basically, what we have here is the same people who still have those Support Our Troops bumper stickers from God knows when, with the American flag on them, encouraging their local police to *shoot* at our troops. So, we designed a new bumper sticker that will fit neatly over their old ones and keep them more current."

A graphic popped up of an old bumper with a new sticker that read, "Support our Troops — With Friendly Fire!"

The audience cheered and applauded. The host said, "Really? You're okay with that? It's not too soon? Okay. I thought it was a little over the top." But he was laughing. Then he added, "Aren't you glad we live in New York? We were the first to voluntarily give up our guns. We're Number One! We're Number One!"

The audience chanted happily along.

Another hostess led off her monologue with, "I considered moving to Texas recently. I mean, think about it: no more IRS." Her audience cheered. "But then I realized they had been replaced by the NRA, and that shooting at our service people was required by law. I mean, it was one thing having that guy in office who bashed the FBI, the Justice Department, the entire intelligence community, and the candidate he had beaten years before. But I draw the line at them demeaning my intelligence by expecting me to shoot at an F-16 with my *six-shooter!*" She pretended to be firing into the sky, along with the requisite, "Pew-pew-pew!" sounds, followed by a "Yee-HAW!"

A third comic took a more somber approach. "Hey, Texas. My father and my brother are both in the United States military. So...fuck you, Texas! I'm glad you're gone!"

He got bleeped — and the loudest ovation of all.

On afternoon cable, Brian Williams kept trying to keep up. "Have you seen the latest? A father in Utah killed his wife and three young children, then himself, in protest over having to give up his guns. He left a note that said, 'I'd rather be dead than unarmed.'"

Williams paused for the irony, then said, "His in-laws, an uncle and aunt of the slain children, said they were appalled at his actions and asked that thoughts and prayers be 'saved for the next murderers.' Powerful words."

He then shifted to another camera. "When we come back, Poland drops all tariffs on small arms shipments to that country, and American gunmakers scramble to ship remaining stocks before they too are seized."

The rush was on.

***

In Idaho, David Billows, Mountain Man, Marjorie, Carlos, and the others watched Williams on satellite while the connection was good. They had taken in three hours of one horrific report after another — crazy people doing crazy shit all over the place, and the federal government having none of it.

As predicted, SAFE was now reaching into rural rebel pockets and a few urban neighborhoods where gun owners — mostly packing unregistered hardware — were holding out, defying GCA, and demonstrating their opposition by getting into firefights.

They were not winning.

Though several SAFE agents — along with ATF and FBI agents, plus some local officers — had given their lives in the take-back program, mostly it was the civilian population taking the losses.

By the most recent count, 357 Americans had chosen fighting and dying to giving up their weapons. Another nine-hundred had been wounded, many of them children caught in the crossfire. To say the program was losing supporters was like saying Hurricane Katrina brought some rain.

Gun collection by SAFE agencies was estimated to have hit 175 million, with about the same to go — if one excluded Texas and Tennessee and took the conservative estimates of overall gun ownership as reliable. Most did not, with some speculation running up to three times that. But the feds were not backing down. A series of commercials had been produced, running throughout the day and night, at taxpayer expense, explaining their position: "Give them up, or we will take them."

All it needed to say.

Still, most Americans seemed pleased since most Americans did not own guns, did not want to own guns and were fine with no one else owning guns. They could easily imagine an America where going to school or to a movie or to a Children's Cancer Hospital was not a dangerous mission.

But the hardliners held strong, producing their own commercials — which ran mainly on NewsMax, OAN, and that new one, not even the craziest QAnon gun nuts watched — that had their own simple message: "Only criminals want illegal guns."

Simple, if not sensible.

But what they were implying — which was easily inferred by their base — was that the government had made guns illegal, and now the government wanted all the illegal guns, ergo the government was just a bunch of criminals coming after *legal* guns.

No one said their base demanded reality — just ire.

When the compound's satellite window closed, and the image slowly merged with static and then became nothing but video noise, Carlos turned it off. Everyone sat in silence for a few moments, then David said to Mountain Man, "Make the call."

Everyone's blood chilled.

As the bearded grizzly bear of a man tried different encrypted satellite phones until he found one that worked, David said to Carlos, "Let's get the vehicles ready."

"Sure thing, boss," Carlos said. Then he repeated, along with David, "And stop calling me 'boss.'"

It broke some of the tension — not with Marjorie or her kids — and David felt it. He gave her a brief if vaguely reassuring smile then started for the door as Carlos opened it and...

...was met by ATF/SAFE Lead Agent Carter Smith.

Smith was backed up by a small army of men in black, complete with balaclavas. They had all three of the compound's guards in zip cuffs, looking piteous.

"Mr. Pillows," Carter Smith said.

David said, "Billows."

"Right. With a B. Sorry." Carter Smith looked past him into the house. "Anyone in here gonna give us any trouble?"

"Depends," David said.

"On?"

"What you want."

"Well, we'll start with your guns, of course. We've got theirs already." He nodded to the abashed guards. "May we come in?"

"Do I have a choice?"

"Sure."

As if on cue, three F-16s were heard approaching, so fast and low that they were over and gone before anyone could clearly see them.

Carter Smith said, "You always have a choice."

David eyed him up and down, then said, "In that case, come in." He stepped aside. "Welcome to our humble abode."

Smith said, "That won't be necessary—the attitude. We come in peace."

"To take our guns."

"That's just the job part. Mind if we look around?" Since that was another *You don't really have a choice* moment, Smith just said, "Thanks."

A slight nod and his team poured in—techy detectors and old school K-9 sniffers.

After they were in and searching, Carter Smith stepped in and shut the door softly behind him. "Coffee?" he asked. When no one offered any, he said, "Okay. Mind if we sit?"

"Who's we?" David said.

"You and I," Carter said.

"I think I'll stand," David said.

"Fine by me," Carter said and took a rocker. He said of

his team, "They'll be quick and neat. We try to be respectful."

David said, "Then you should respect the right of all Americans to own and possess firearms."

Smith said, "Yeah, well, you don't *have* that right anymore, thanks to *your* Congress." He was not open to having that discussion again in his lifetime.

David decided to sit. He drew a chair up to face Agent Smith. "You're pretty brave. In here with us, alone."

"Not really," Smith said. "Semper Fi."

He rolled up his sleeve to reveal a Corps tattoo on his forearm that almost precisely matched the one on David's shoulder, which he did not offer to reveal. Instead, he said, "There are some crazy ex-marines out there."

"There are," Smith said. "And I'm here to find out if you're one of them." He paused, then asked, "Are you one of them, David?"

"I have my moments," he said.

"Don't we all," Carter Smith said, and threw an empty chuckle. He took out his business card and handed it over. "If you decide you have anything you want to tell me."

David read the card and asked, "What's the 'C' stand for?"

"Carter," Smith said. "Carter Carter Smith."

"I'm sorry," David said.

"My parents had a strange sense of humor," Smith said. "They each had a grandfather named Carter, ironically enough. So...." He nodded at the card. David set it aside on an end table, and Carter Smith cut to the chase. "We hear you might want to kill the president."

"Who says?"

"You do," Smith said. When David gave up the tiniest bit of surprise and confusion, Smith said, "We've had you bugged for six months."

If David had been more transparent with his emotions, his jaw might have dropped. But in his line of work, he knew anything was possible. The question was: Who was the mole?

He looked around the room until his eyes found Mountain Man, head hung slightly. "Sorry, David," he said. "Just business. Nothing personal. I like you, man."

He stood and walked out.

Carter Smith looked to see if anyone would pull a concealed weapon and shoot the big burly guy in the back, but no one showed any more than muted disgust and regret.

Smith said to David, "Like he said, sorry about that. Just business. We had enough on him to put him away for the rest of his life and ten more. Don't blame him."

David said stoically, "I don't blame anyone anymore."

"Good way to be these days," Smith said. Then he nodded toward the door and said, "I see you've got a track hoe out there."

David said only, "Septic issues."

Smith nodded. "So, you're not planning to knock down any walls, say in D.C. Crash through to perform some heroic deed in the name of false patriotism."

David let him finish, then said, "No."

"Good," Smith said. "I'll take your word on that." But he added, "So, no plans for violence against our government."

"I thought you said you'd take my word for it."

"I need to hear you say it — so that we're clear."

David nodded and said, "None foreseen in the immediate future."

Carter Smith chuckled honestly — a rarer event these days — and said, "Okay."

As his agents returned, their coffers filled to the brim with weapons and ammo, Carter Smith stood and said, "Whoa. A bonanza." But as they carried their caches outside, Smith said to David, who had also stood, "To tell the truth, I expected more."

"Outside," David said, to the point.

"Of course," Smith said, certain that his people had located and confiscated them all by now.

As he started to turn for the door, he felt David's hand on his arm. He looked back into the stern face of a former fellow jarhead, who tapped his tattoo and said, "How'd that work out for you?"

Smith looked down a beat, then back up. "You take an oath, and it's for life. Doesn't go away just because you change careers." He looked David dead in the eye. "I got this great new job with the Bureau to protect citizens' rights and freedoms. Now everyone wants to kill me for taking their guns. You?"

David almost smiled, then said, "I'm doin' okay."

"Good," Smith said. "Okay, is good."

As they stepped outside, David could see Mountain Man in the back of one of the black SUVs looking remorseful, but he chose not to return the look or comment. Smith noted the non-exchange and said to David, "So...we're good here? No need to come back?"

"I wouldn't bother — if I was you," David said.

Smith nodded and looked around. "Nice place you got. Kinda lonely, but I suppose that's the point." When David did not respond, Smith said, "I understand you were motor pool in the Sandpit — before you volunteered for Korengal. Not many guys would pick a place like that."

"I'm not many guys," David said. "Just me."

"Get many righteous kills there?" Smith said.

"Enough," David said.

Smith nodded. "But you're still a mechanic."

"You heard that, too?"

Smith nodded. "Thing is, I've got this 2014 Subaru Outback. It's making this ticking sound somewhere inside the motor or transmission. Maybe the ignition system. I can't tell. Like a...*tick-tick-tack* kinda sound. You have any thoughts on that?"

David shook his head. "You're on your own, there. I don't do foreign stuff."

Smith looked into David Billows' eyes longer than anyone else would have expected, but neither man thought it unusual, nor did they flinch. Finally, Smith turned away and called out to his second-in-command: "Are we clear? All the outbuildings?"

"We're good to go, Chief," the man said.

Carter C. Smith turned back to David. "Okay, then. Sorry for the intrusion. You have a nice rest of your day." He turned away, then turned back. "And good luck, Captain."

"You too, Agent," David said.

Smith nodded, turned away, got in the lead SUV, and his team sped off into the verdant Colorado mountains. David watched them go, never taking his eyes off Mountain Man, who returned the gaze until the canyon boulders came between them.

At that point, David stepped back inside and ordered Carlos to "Sweep it."

Carlos had swept for bugs earlier in the day and had not found any. Mountain Man had been the mole. He *was* the bug. Now he was now gone, and the place was clean, most likely. In the end, in the coming end, it would not matter.

"Are we all good?" David asked the remaining crew.

Everyone said they were, and he believed them. The danger had passed.

Now, they could get on with their plans.

CHAPTER SEVENTEEN

Nineteen different prepper compounds were attacked in Idaho alone— "attacked" being the term of choice for non-reporters on the Big Blue-F Channel. "That is really disturbing footage," Friendly Foxer Frank Fitzsimmons said, scowling appropriately. "These were peaceful people forced into a situation of defending themselves against our own government."

"Right here in America," Eva Beverly parroted. "Land of the free."

"And home of the brave."

"They were very brave. Very, very brave."

"It's frightening."

"*So* frightening."

"It is, Eva. In other similar situations— some *eight hundred* of them—where government-identified 'militants' said they would peacefully hand over their weapons, *nothing happened*. Nothing at all!"

"That is so shocking. I am…in shock."

Shockingly shocked she was. But there was some truth in Fitzsimmons' numerical recap. Over seven-hundred loudmouthed militant groups identified by the government and the Southern Poverty Law Center for their self-identified social media and real-life militant activities did choose discretion over valor and, when surrounded, said, "Come on in." Perhaps not happily so, but they gave up their guns and for that sacrifice were alive.

In other parts of Idaho, nineteen compounds held their ground to tragic results. SAFE agents had the law on their side when anyone opened fire on them, with the power to use any force necessary to protect themselves, others in the area, or simply to uphold the law itself.

So in Idaho, Missouri, Arkansas, Georgia, the Dakotas, and even California — central California — when SAFE agents came knockin' and the "Patriot Militias" started rockin' their ARs, S&Ws, Remingtons, and Colts — whatever had ammo in it — SAFE agents did whatever was deemed necessary by their Agent in Charge.

Apparently, many Seconders, as they came to be called, had not learned from the Big Angie Miller and Montana compound episodes. As a result, most of the later compounds were leveled, usually by armor-clad bulldozers, occasionally by airpower, once by heavy artillery, and twice by tanks that were brought in more as a threat — one that was ignored.

Entire families died thanks to their belligerent patriarchs.

Collateral damage was common in war, just not in America. But GCA was war. There was no more doubting it. When Air National Guard jets dropped smart ordnance into the homes of outliers and rebels, often into their mini rogue states — some had their own flags — outrage was sure to follow. And FoxNews was not alone.

Within weeks, all the major news outlets — broadcast, cable, and web-based — were running footage showing the aftermath of the compound "entries" — now uniformly referred to as "raids" and "attacks." SAFE provided information on casualties and tried to offset those chilling stats with background on the nutcases who brought on the firefights. But in the end, it was the graphic footage of dead children that held America's attention.

SAFE leader Carter Smith did his best to downplay the bloodshed.

"We gave ample warning and clearly advised the residents of the compound to, at the very least, let the children go. But they chose to use their own children as shields, cowardly hiding behind infants in the belief that firing on authorized federal agents complying with every applicable law would not result in them taking every legal counterventive action available. Though we are deeply saddened at this entirely unnecessary loss of life, whatever the victims' ages, we must remind the American public that these self-described rogues and law deniers have brought these horrors on themselves. We regret our parts in these sad events but also remind the public that we do not, under any circumstances, ever fire the first shot, and hold off as long as we can. However, if you continue to fire at us, we will return fire—until we receive no further resistance, whatever the stakes, regrettably."

Smith gave that press conference a few weeks in—before his teams lit up the nearly fifty "resistance compounds" nationwide.

Before the outrage.

Privately, he expressed tremendous grief. This was not what he had signed on for, as he often said, but it was his job. He had taken that one oath and was now stuck with it. "To defend and protect" had morphed into "disarm or incapacitate." When he left Iraq, he figured he was done killing. He could never have imagined in a hundred tours that he would be killing American citizens as part of his job description.

Carter Smith was unnerved and cried in private on more than one occasion.

But he often used his visit to David Billows' compound as a case example of how it all was supposed to work. Though there they had caught his guards by surprise and were able to peacefully remove their weapons without firing a shot, the "without firing a shot" part was what mattered, as he saw it.

"These entries should be peaceful," was his point, "Must be peaceful," his mantra. If his team could enter a compound like that one, with as many weapons and as much malintent as had been reported, then they could enter any other compound with similar non-dramatic effects.

That was what he promoted, and in most cases, nothing did happen. But peaceful encounters did not get reported. Where was the news/shock value in those headlines? "SAFE agents enter militia compound, and nothing happens!" So very blah. Carter Smith had been on more than one confiscation entry at a "heavily-armed-insurrection center" where the militants ended up shaking hands with the agents, thanking them for being so professional, and even sharing stories, jokes, and a beer.

But as more entries went bad and the "raid" videos went viral, even Carter Smith had to remind himself that there would come an end to this madness, someday; eventually SAFE would route out every defiant gun-loving kook — whether he thought he was a patriot or knew he was just a kook — and take his guns, making America safer with each action. In the meantime, FoxNews folks were having a *blast*.

"Have you seen this latest footage of an attack in Maryland?"

"Maryland. That's *close*."

"Unimaginable that they would kill so many peaceful patriots."

"Only defending themselves."

"That's it."

"The best defense is a good offense."

"And this is offensive as hell."

"You betcha."

"Just brutal outright murder if you ask me."

"I didn't, but I will."

"Brutal."

"Murder."

"Outright."

"Thoughts and prayers."

What was truly brutal, prayer-wise, was the TV preachers elbowing each other out of the way to get in on the solicitation action. One of them got so carried away, he shot himself by accident.

Standing before a giant map of America, he was on fire, oratorically. "*Jee*-sus said, let there be a *hell*fire rain of truth on the infidels! I say *storm* the rancid temples of government and smite those with extreme prejudice who might dare take our guns and our religious freedoms for the evil stink of homosexual communism in America! The heathen pederasts and trans-defigured molesters will be run from our public toilets like the swarthy money changers by our Lord and God *Jee*-sus. Like the dangerous vermin they are! The perverted genitalia-lovers must face their fate NOW! Death to the homo-centric America we have lost!"

With that, he lifted a nickel-plated pocket rocket—he called it his Roy Moralizer—waved it around, and shot the map until he was out of bullets.

Or so he thought.

"Burn in *Hell*, America!" he shouted as he took out a lighter and set the map on fire in several spots across the bottom. In seconds, the entire map was ablaze, and seconds after that, his church.

Jumping away, terrified, his hand jerked, and that last round he did not know he had in the chamber received the firing pin, sending the bullet into his knee. The last words heard before the video went dead — apparently on fire — were, "Holy shit! Someone call 9-1-1!" And there was the "Owwww. Fuck me, Satan!" of course.

He was not arrested for having the gun, though it was confiscated, and he was provided prompt medical help by two gay EMTs, who likely saved his life as he had nicked an artery. But the rural volunteer fire department was unable to save his church, which burned to the ground along with his adjoining house.

His insurance agent later told him, in the hospital, that he was not covered for fires set on his premises by his own hand. "It's kinda like arson, Robbie," was what the Allstate guy said before asking him if he wanted to press charges against himself from his hospital bed. The Reverend RJ Jones said he did not because he was still trying to figure out how he was going to pay for his stay in the ICU.

Like Big Angie Miller before him, he too had refused Obamacare — on principle.

The story did not run on right wing propaganda stations, but Jake Tapper had fun with it — before getting to the serious side of non-peaceful resistance.

Even Jake was appalled.

CHAPTER EIGHTEEN

Around the country, protests had begun against the "murder" of innocent resisters. Even the Parkland School survivors/anti-gun activists — four of them now in Congress — were showing signs of Raid Fatigue, as it had been dubbed. The Westboro bunch made new signs proclaiming that all the children had been murdered because of homosexuals, fornicators, and fruit-at-the-bottom yogurt.

Their message was, as usual, mixed.

In the not-so-sovereign — and now losing money like a Trump casino — former state of Tennessee, snake handlers were debating whether such an enterprise was still wise, given that they had more guns than congregants in their houses of worship.

Sheds.

Down in Florida, south of Ocala in Ocklawaha, some lunatic with Confederate flags and one stolen Jefferson Davis monument — he said "rescued" — had hung two mannequins from a live oak tree in his front yard, next to one of six metal sheds from Home Depot, and dangerously close to his single wide in an area known for tornadic activity, as the Weather Channel continually warned.

He had painted one of the mannequins a dark tan and

hung a placard around its neck that read "Nunca Navarro," even though he likely *never* would run for anything ever again. The other one was spray-painted black with a sign that read President Pinko. Underneath them sat a crudely manufactured red, white, and blue gravestone—probably a leftover Halloween decoration from decades before bought at a neighbor's yard sale for a dollar—that read R.I.P. Amerca.

Plastic gravestones not supporting spellcheck.

When one of the SAFE agents looked closely, he could see that Peace had originally been spelled Piece but had been painted over—twice.

Peice.

The lead SAFE agent, a stout but taut Hispanic woman named Sara Rios, called out over a megaphone. "Mr. Cuatrel, please come out without a disturbance. We are only here to confiscate your weapons, not to harm you in any way. Just open the door and show us your empty hands, please."

This precaution was being taken because Cuatrel had been featured on a local television show, a short piece on the News at Noon, saying that "they" were going to have to come and pry open his cold, dead, etc., etc. He ended with, "Come and get me. Just try!" before throwing in a plural N-word casually if vitriolically, then going on to imply some vague conspiracy between Mexicans, Muslims, "Chinee," and "the" Jews.

To cover his bases.

"We don't aim to harm you in any way, Mr. Cuatrel," SAFE agent Rios said into her megaphone. "So please, just step outside slowly and show us your hands."

A moment later, the trailer door cracked open, and a rusty five-iron with a yellowed handkerchief poked out and jiggled around.

"We see the flag, sir. Just come on out slowly. We won't

shoot."

Sara Rios was a beacon of calm. She had been doing this for almost six weeks and had seen it all, by her own estimation. She was wrong.

"All right, I'm comin' out," was heard from inside the trailer.

"Are you alone in there, sir?" Rios asked.

"Just me an' my shadow," Cuatrel muttered.

"Is your shadow a person or just an actual shadow, sir?" Sara asked.

"Huh?"

She shared a shaking head, eyes rolling look with her number two, a guy everyone called Buddy even though his given name was John Arthur Simms, and said through the megaphone, "Just come on, then."

By that point, most of Cuatrel's neighbors had come out to look but were being kept at a safe distance by agents and police in case Mr. Cuatrel opted to make good on his promise. The jaundiced white flag fell to the ground, Carl "Tommy" Cuatrel stuck both his hands out and waved them around, then he stepped out…naked.

"Ain't got no guns on me, see?" He turned slowly around to face forward again. "They're all inside on the living room floor, ready for you. You won't have to look for 'em, less you want to."

Agent Rios lowered her megaphone. "Thank you, sir. But you didn't have to remove your clothing for us."

"Didn't wanna get shot, someone thinkin' I had a gun hidden."

One of the agents leaned to another and said, "He could have a few up under there."

"Hidden in all that fur," the other said.

Cuatrel was an overweight and hirsute individual, it was true.

As the agents eased past him, carefully avoiding contact, Mr. Cuatrel stood still with his hands in the air and asked Rios, "Can I at least keep *them*?"

He nodded toward his offensive mannequins.

Sarah Rios said, "Yes, sir. Those are covered under Free Speech."

"At least we still got one amendment left," he grumbled.

"And a few others," Rios pointed out. Which brought only another grumble. Agent Rios then turned to the rookie on their team, a pretty black woman who had just turned twenty-two, and said, "DiWanna, keep an eye on him, would you?"

When Agent DiWanna Tiller did not move, Rios added, "Up there."

On the stoop with Cuatrel.

DiWanna reluctantly stepped up onto the narrow porch, doing her best to conceal her repugnance—not an entirely successful gambit. As Rios went past them, headed inside to supervise, with a grin a mile wide, Cuatrel turned to the young African American agent and said, "You gonna arrest me, honey? We could have a helluva good time lookin' for the soap!" He raised his eyebrows a few times.

Though she tried not to look, DiWanna Tiller could tell that her charge was getting an erection, and she wondered what she had gotten herself into with this damned new job. She also had no idea her peripheral vision was so damned good.

She was cursed for sure.

While entries into places like "Cuatrel's Trailers," as they came to be called by the SAFE teams, were not the norm, humorous encounters were not uncommon. Some folks were relieved to hear a joke made to defuse the situation and laughed harder than they normally might simply to allay the anxiety.

And, for the most part, the gun-removal program progressed on schedule, with the volume of retrieved weapons updated hourly on the GCA website. That latest claimed that 219,345,676 guns had been taken off the streets of America.

"Gone for *good!*" as the new billboards said.

But it was not all good, as Brian Williams reported. "A startling development today in the government's Operation Fierce Freedom, implementing the Gun Care Act."

Footage of several buildings on fire came up.

"A group of fundamentalist survivalist-doomsdayers in New Mexico burned their own compound rather than give up, as their leader David Yosarian said, 'Their God-given right to guns and self-governance' — and self-immolation it would seem."

Williams loved his little dark asides.

First, no one had reported that the SAFE program was known internally as Operation Fierce Freedom. NBC got the scoop on that one from a disgruntled GCA middle-management type let go for constantly bitching and whining about the "loss of Second Amendment protection" while he was supposed to be managing the website update number.

Second, the New Mexico compound was burning like hell in the video made by the Las Cruces Fire Department, whose members had not even attempted to put out the intense blaze, which gave new scope to the term "fully involved." There were not enough hoses in the state, nor water in the Rio Grande, to put out that fire.

Williams read words that appeared on the screen in a

box and quotes. "In a statement released just before he set the compound afire, Yosarian said, 'The rogue nations [*sic*] of America will not take our guns. God will judge those who smote us with flames.'"

Williams came back on screen to say, "And with that, he lit the fire that killed seventy-six adults, thirty-seven children, and 114 animals. We'll have more on Operation Fierce Freedom after the break."

Thinking he was clear, Williams added off-camera, "Operation Fierce Freedom. Who comes up with this crap?"

America heard.

In the White House, President Roger Pinkins was asking the same question—with more volume—of his chief of staff, Henry Hillerman. "Who the *hell* came up with Operation Fierce Freedom? That is by far the stupidest name for a massive movement against the people of the United States that I have ever heard! It's worse than calling the law itself the Gun Care Act! Speaking of which, who the hell came up with THAT?!"

"I believe it was Carter Smith's number two."

"Have we fired him yet?"

"Her. And no, she's on the front line, serving with gusto."

"Gusto," Pinkins said, shaking his head. "Disarming America with Gusto. Now *there's* a slogan."

"I like it."

The president had been poring over reports from various raids—both successful and not—and stopped on a photo of nude Cuatrel standing on his stoop by a distressed DiWanna Tiller, "Amerca's" gravestone, and the two mannequins prominent in the foreground.

Pinkins asked, "Did he at least take the dummies down?"

Hillerman chuckled. "Nope. Still hangin'."

Pinkins groaned. "I suppose we have bigger fish to fry. What happened in the House today?"

"Couple of bills I'm sure you'll love."

"Dear God," Pinkins moaned. "How do those morons have the nerve to go home to their districts on the weekend?"

"Most of them don't," Henry said. "And those who do don't mention what they're doing back here."

"Maybe they aren't as dumb as I imagine."

"I doubt it."

"So, what will I be vetoing next week?"

"First one, House Bill 3729-B, is calling for anyone who knows that someone else has a gun and doesn't report it to get a mandatory five years, hard."

"That sounds a bit harsh."

"Whip Meyers is trying to talk them down to two."

"Generous. Do we think it will pass?"

"Probably not. They just want to look like they're doing something."

"That's a high bar. What else?"

"Tom Briggs with the Patriot's Circus—uh, *Caucus*—is circulating a bill that will fund the building of a statue of every member of the House and Senate in their hometowns. Check out this language." Henry Hillerman read, "'The head of each Congressional committee shall receive funding for a statue of their personal likeness in the town of their choosing in the state of their most recent elective victory.'"

"Dear Jesus on a stick. How much?"

"Million-four each."

Pinkins threw his head back as if his neck had just broken. When he looked back, jaw open for a moment, he said, "And the chances of that one passing?"

"Close to a hundred percent. They highly admire

themselves and their few accomplishments."

"Veto."

"Yes, sir."

"What else?"

"Helen Conners over in the Senate has suggested legislation that would make it illegal to threaten killing you or anyone in Congress."

"Isn't that already a law?"

"Not specifically. It's kind of a grey area."

"And they mean to make it canonical."

"They figure it can't hurt."

"Can they include late night comedians?"

"I'll look into it."

"Those bastards."

"Did you see Kimmell last night? Criminy. He was on a rip."

"I try to be in bed before the slaughter begins. Anything else?"

"Kate Callooley from St. Paul would like a photo op for her pet cause."

"Which is?"

"Um, pets. Actual pets."

"What's the cause?"

"Honoring them."

"Honoring…. For what?"

"Being pets. It's just one picture so she can Instagram it to all the pet owners in Minnesota. It's a campaign thing."

"Ya think?" Pinkins said, and dropped his head to his desk. When he looked up, he said, "You know, if anyone had told me I'd be dealing with this much pathetic bullcrap every goddamned day, I'd have stayed home in Wichita." Then he warned Henry, "And please spare me the Glen Campbell joke this one time. I'm not in the mood."

"Yes, sir. No, sir."

"Why do I keep you around?"

"Because I keep the really creepy senators out of your office, and you secretly love my Glen Campbell jokes."

"He died of Alzheimer's, you know."

"No, I forgot."

"Ha-ha-ha. Goodnight, Gracie." Pinkins stood.

Hillerman said, "Oh. One other thing. I almost forgot. And this is the most important of all."

"I can hardly wait," Pinkins said, and made a twelve-second call to his wife upstairs, telling her that he was on his way. "If I can get rid of Henry."

He hung up, and Henry told him, "Mel LaFlore is shopping an idea around the House that seems to be gaining some traction. I think it might have legs."

"What is it?"

"A memorial to all those who died refusing to give up their guns."

Pinkins pulled back a moment, thought it over, then said, "Tell me more."

"The idea is simple — kind of like Mel. But brilliant, I might add — in this case. Mel wants to build a tower, five-sided — like the old Chrysler logo…you know, on their old cars, those little vans, but taller, and narrow at the top — with the names of all the Americans who sacrificed their lives defending themselves from the Gun Care Act engraved into the sides."

"How many names?"

"We're up to just over four hundred. We do not anticipate more than a few hundred more before it's over. Thousand, tops."

"Cost?"

"Meh," Hillerman said. "Two-three million. Five, maybe, figuring in graft and political favors. Mel owes a lot of people. But I think it's worth every penny. It should get your numbers up at least a point for every hundred dead that stood up to Operation Fierce Freedom and gave their lives, rather than cave in to the federal government's demands to give up their Second Amendment-protected right to own firearms."

"Former amendment."

"Exactly my point."

"It's a 'cake and eat it too' deal."

"Couldn't have said it better myself, sir."

"Tell 'em to have it on my desk as soon as it's in decent shape so we can start getting the word out."

And so the wheels of government turned, slowly but inefficiently, with the always laser-like focus on optics over conscience, just as the forefathers did not intend — even if they did want a well-regulated militia should England reverse-invade us again.

At least most of what was going on was out in the open. Pinkins was a big believer in transparency — providing he looked good standing behind the glass and had his nice suit on.

Of course, not *everything* was out in the open.

***

Down in the abandoned federal building basement, ex-sergeant Mike Cho came into Harris Ball's lair to update him on all that was happening around the nation — everything that had nothing to do with Congress.

"Ah, Mr. Cho," Ball said. "How goes things?"

"Well, sir."

"Cho...."

"Sorry. Old training dies hard."

"Lay it on me."

"The Westboro Church walking loony bin is planning a march on Washington to protest 'the godless state of faggery in D.C.,' I believe is how they put it."

"Beautiful, beautiful. Anyone else buying into it?"

"Not because of them, directly, but yes, we're anticipating the excitement will spread. We've sent out emails and brochures, dropped pamphlets, saturated Reddit, Twitter, Facebook, Instagram, TextMe, Trampl. Fidgit, the whole lot of them."

"Good, good. Perfect. Gotta love the fine points of AgitProp. What's our theme?"

"Take America Back."

"Not very original."

"It never is, sir. Not if it's going to be effective," Cho said.

Ball said, "Have all of our people been put on notice?"

"I believe so, sir. Sorry."

Ball let it go. "Date set?"

"To coincide with the march, as soon as they firm up their plans. Looks to be the fifteenth."

Ball leaned over to check a calendar and do some quick calculations. "Perfect. Bring 'em in."

"Everyone?"

"Everyone."

"On the fifteenth?"

"Night of the fourteenth."

"Got it, sir."

Cho turned to go. Ball said, "Hey, Mike. I ever tell you you remind me of the worst Chinese waiter I ever had? Name was Kimchi, I think."

Cho, who was Korean American, said, "Fuck you, you racist asshole."

"Thatta boy!"

Mike Cho's boss had a hearty laugh and went back to his WSJ opinion piece about the real reason behind Operation Fierce Freedom and the GCA, but he could find no point being made other than it was about to all come crumbling down.

"Which is the point," Ball said to himself, and lit a fresh cigar even though the last one was only half-smoked and still lit.

Harris Ball was in a mood to celebrate.

CHAPTER NINETEEN

On Fox's friendliest show, Frank and Eva had been laughing one moment about an animal segment— "Did you hear that Panda burp?" "I sure did. He must be a liberal." "*Very* liberal!" Ha-ha-ha!—straight into, "On a more serious note, for those of you who still have your guns, a disturbing turn of events has caused alarm in Miami."

Eva finished Frank's lead-in. "What has been called the safest school in America…is safe no more."

"Not safe at all, Eva. Not safe—at *all*."

What they were jabbering about had taken place in South Miami-Dade, down past Perrine, earlier in the day when SAFE agents, led personally by Carter Smith, came to the Ruger S. Sauer Elementary School, which had been dubbed by its principal Jonah T. Darwin, an ex-marine, America's Safest School.

There were reasons for the claim.

First were the double concrete walls—twenty-feet of concrete, thirty-feet apart, topped with razor wire that sandwiched two inner fifteen-foot walls made entirely of razor wire. Surrounding it all was a "perimeter wire" a hundred feet out. Basically: more razor wire.

No one was getting in—or out.

Four guard towers rose, one at each corner of the compound, with two former Navy Seals in each air-conditioned, armor plate-walled turrets, narrow gun-slots allowing Sauer's snipers to aim at any point inside or outside the double-double walls of the elementary school. Each turret was outfitted with assault rifles—fully automatic, laser guided—starlight glasses for night school, RPGs—drive-by deterrents—and one case of Soviet-era hand grenades.

But what made this K-6 school remarkable in the self-defense arena were its twin tanks. Principal Darwin had raised sufficient funds to purchase them from military salvage dealers overseas, have them imported as "museum" pieces, then retrofitted to "active firepower status." I.e., they worked. "Full wartime functionality" was the certification. He had a third on order.

As Carter Smith and his small fleet of black SUVs entered through the perimeter-wire main gate, where parents drove in to drop off their kids, both tank muzzles swung around to aim at the orderly column of intruders. No one fired.

Yet.

When Smith got out of his vehicle, he was "greeted" by Darwin himself—a stocky barrel of a man with more bravado than humanity, a buzz cut, and full fatigues with service medals galore. After Smith introduced himself pleasantly, as always, Principal Darwin saluted, stiff as a plank, and held out his hand—not to shake, but an order for Carter to "Halt."

Ever the calmest man in the situation, Smith said, "Okay," and halted.

Most of the other agents had climbed out of their vehicles, leaving the dogs in the A/C for now, cars idling—and not just because it was Miami and already hot as Hades, but common-sense standard police operating procedure.

Nobody wanted to see Rover vaporized by a tank round.

Darwin said, "You must surrender your weapon, sir, and submit to a full body search, then pass through the scanners — the wand and the tunnel. Inside, you will be given another body search by hand. If you do not agree to these conditions, you may not enter Ruger S. Sauer Elementary School, the Safest School in America. Because we *are* the safest school in America."

Above Principal Darwin's head, seven huge American flags swayed gently, framed against a deep blue sky dotted with typically low and white idly-drifting South Florida powder puff clouds — Carter Smith thinking it would be poetic, somehow, if it wasn't so patriotically pretentions and patently dumb.

Smith looked up, then back down and said, "So we've heard."

"What have you heard?" Darwin wanted to know. He seemed edgy, putting his hand on the butt of his hip-holstered .45.

"Everything you wanted us to hear, Mr. Darwin," Smith said.

"I prefer Colonel Darwin," civilian Darwin said.

"Sure," Smith said diplomatically — and nothing else.

Darwin's face fell. He said, "You'll have to remove the vest, too."

"And why would that be?"

"Because we *are* the safest school in America." He added, "It sends the wrong message." He stuck out his jaw as if he were mimicking George C. Scott mimicking Patton.

"I would have guessed it was something else," Smith said, glancing around at the forward base protocols. He said, "What about me? Am *I* safe if someone decides to shoot me?"

Darwin assured him that that would not happen "in my school."

Smith read between his lines and said, "Just don't try to take your guns."

"No sir," Darwin said cheerily and woefully at the same time. "That would not be a good idea." Then he said, "You can keep your earpiece if you like. We don't want you to feel threatened or out of contact with your platoon."

Smith repeated, "Platoon."

Darwin said: "The vest." It was not a question but more of a command.

Maybe a commandment.

Carter thanked Darwin for being allowed to keep his earpiece in, then took off his vest in the spirit of compromise and lubrication of an uneasy state of affairs—as well as its uneasy head of state. In doing so, Smith revealed his Marine Corps tat.

Colonel Darwin said, "Semper Fi. Any guns?"

"Nope," Smith said, half-expecting some attempt at a secret handshake. The way he said it. "I don't customarily need a weapon, Mr. Darwin. Semper Fi."

Darwin squinted at the diminution and said, "We'll see."

Smith understood him to mean not that "we'll see" if Smith might need a gun, but that he might have one, concealed, and Darwin's stooges would be certain to find it.

"This way," Darwin said, then nodded back. "Everyone else stays out here."

"For now," Smith said.

"Forever," Darwin said.

Smith snuck a glance at his number two on this mission, Sara Rios, from the original Cautrel's Trailer episode. One of the tank commanders and his gunner, up top, saw it and seemed to think it was a smirk, so the gunner shadowed Carter Smith with the fifty.

Through the steel doors of the concrete walls and slipway between the concertina wire walls between them went Darwin then Smith, Carter saying, "These are quite the precautions."

He did not say *for an elementary school.*

Darwin would not have cared. He said, "You ain't seen nothin' yet, Agent Smith."

At what was apparently the only entrance to the school building, a dozen well-armed men in full SWAT gear lined a narrow hallway of bulletproof Plexiglas, at the end of which was an elaborately mechanized steel door, half-a-foot thick. As he stepped through the one-man-wide corridor, Smith wondered, "Where'd you get the money for all this, Colonel?"

"Bebe Rebozo," Darwin said sarcastically and otherwise did not answer the question. He then stopped and said, "Stop here."

Carter stopped, and a Kevlar'd, face-masked SWAT guy carefully and slowly ran a metal-detector wand over every inch of the lead SAFE agent's body, including his head.

"Okay," Darwin said when nothing beeped, and walked through the metal detector, setting it off. He said back over his shoulder, "Through here." Carter Smith walked through, and Darwin said, "And here," where another person — possibly a woman — gave Smith another slow once-over with *her* wand, including his head again. That done, Darwin said, "In there, and it's over."

He indicated a Plexi'd room where a woman waited to do a hands-on body search. Carter knew this because she was wearing blue TSA gloves and a dour expression. With blonde and braided pigtails and black-rimmed glasses, she called to mind *Ilsa, She Wolf of the SS*. Smith imagined her technique would match her countenance.

Carter asked Darwin if the children had to go through this, and, as the fruit-salad principal/colonel walked ahead through the last set of bulletproof glass doors, he said, "Every day. That's why we're the safest school in—"

The closing door cut him off as *Ilsa* thoroughly felt all over Carter's body, somehow managing to get a finger halfway up his rectal cavity through his pants.

She was a pro.

When Carter came out on the other side of the explosion-resistant doors, Darwin was gone. A ready-for-battle dude with sergeant stripes and a long-fixed glower said, "This way," and led Carter down a hallway to the first door.

"In there," he said, and turned to stiffly stand guard, responding to Smith's "Thank you, Sergeant" by closing and locking the door behind him.

Carter grunted amazement, shook his head once, then turned to face a woman of thirty-five or so—stocky, strong-willed, and overly blonde—who was also packing. Hers was an H&K Sig .40, holstered on her hip, but her AR was not far away, leaning against her desk.

"Agent Smith, I'm Karen Schmulberg. Welcome to Ruger S. Sauer School." She did not add the usual laudatory addendum, thankfully. One more time, and Carter Smith was asking for his gun back.

Karen Schmulberg extended her hand to shake, and Smith accepted it—her grip was extra firm. He said, "Please to meet you, Ms. Schmulberg. This is your classroom?"

"Yes, it is."

"What grade do you teach?"

"Second grade, sir. Best class of second graders I've ever had," she said, sounding like R. Lee Ermey in *Full Metal Jacket*.

"You don't have to call me 'sir,'" Smith said.

"Okay, I won't," she said.

Smith smiled and looked around the room at the thirty or so tiny desks. "Where are they today?"

"Dismissed until this issue is worked out."

"GCA," Carter said.

"If that stands for Grab the Country of America."

Carter maintained his smile. "Ms. Schmulberg, I'm just here to do my job. So, why don't you explain your method. Maybe we can work something out."

She said, "There's nothing to work out. We teach our kids and keep them safe while we're at it."

"Safest school in America," Smith said, deciding to give it a whirl, then further deciding it sounded even more ridiculous dripping off his tongue.

Karen did not hear it that way. "Damn right," she said. "We earned it."

He said, "At some mighty cost to some anonymous investors, it appears."

Karen Schmulberg said nothing.

Carter Smith said, "So…." And he looked around. "How's it work? I assume it's the same for all classes in all grades."

"Consistency is safety," Schmulberg said with surety.

Smith looked to see if the slogan was printed on a colorful banner hung like kiddie crown molding. It was. He said, "Walk me through it. Pretend I'm a concerned parent."

"Our parents aren't concerned. They're assured."

"Right. So…." He lowered himself into one of the tiny desks to watch.

Schmulberg sucked at a molar and turned away, apparently deciding to play along for now. She said, "Every day, the kids come through the one entrance, same as you did.

They get the wand, then they're frisked, X-rayed, scanned, and frisked again."

Remembering Ilsa's finger in his ass, Carson said, "Body searching children. Parents okay with that?"

Schmulberg said, "They're okay with anything that keeps their kids safe."

"No one gets in here but the staff and the kids," he said.

"Not a one," she said, and opened a standard-issue elementary school teacher's tall cabinet, the difference being that this one contained a floor-to-ceiling rack of small-caliber handguns, five-shot .22s. She said, "Once the children are in their seats, I hand these out."

"Loaded," Smith said.

"Of course," Schmulberg said. "What would be the point otherwise?" It appeared that she was barely able to refrain from saying something like, *The only way to stop a bad guy with a gun is a good second-grader with a loaded .22 caliber hand weapon.*

And that she would expect more than an apple for having said it.

Smith said, "You're not worried about...accidental shootings?"

"The children are well-trained in gun safety."

"No accidents yet."

"No accidents ever."

"Okay," Carter said, already not doing a great job of disguising his doubt and cynicism. "What's next? Lessons, one would presume."

Schmulberg had missed none of what he was trying so poorly trying to hide. "I don't care for your attitude, Agent Smith. What we are doing here is the future of education."

"I hope not, Ms. Schmulberg," he said. "But please, continue."

She bit her tongue and said, "Yes. Lessons. English. Math. Science. Drawing." She spat it all out almost as one word, possibly implying that all of it was secondary to marksmanship.

Smith said, "Drawing?"

"Of course," teacher Schmulberg said. "Art is an important facet of the enriched young mind."

"Right," Agent Smith said. "And then?"

"Bible study," she said, *glaring*, he thought, no doubt guessing what this government secularist thought of *that*.

In his inimitable darkly plain style, Carter Smith said, "Of course." And changed the subject. "I noticed that the bathrooms across the hall are padlocked. What if the kids have to, you know — go?"

Schmulberg nodded to a trash can in the corner. "Then they use the latrine bucket."

"Latrine bucket?" Smith said of the standard-issue elementary school teacher's trash pale — grey, thin-sided, short. He looked back. "They use it...in front of everyone else?"

"They learn not to be bashful, and the children all turn their heads," Karen said, as if reading from a memorized script.

Carter intuited a glitch. "But *you* don't turn away. In case there's a...an intruder."

"Someone sneaking into class with a weapon, yes," she said.

"With all that out there? How would they do that?"

"They won't," she said.

"But you watch the kids pee, anyway. Or...whatever else they have to do. In the can."

"It's not my favorite part of the job," Karen Schmulberg

admitted. "But it's necessary."

Carson wondered, "Who…empties that trash can?"

Karen nodded toward the bulletproof glass in the door and said, "Mr. Jenkins, our custodial engineer."

Smith looked out the window into the hallway, where he could see an older black man, Jacob Johnson "Three Jay" Jenkins, shaking his head. Clearly, he did not care for that part of his new job duties either.

He walked away, still shaking his head.

Carter Smith's guardian sergeant kept a keen eye on Jenkins, then turned his eyes back to fix on Carter, who said to Karen Schmulberg, "My keeper seems a little intense."

To which Karen Schmulberg said, "He's been thoroughly vetted, I assure you. United States Army, Oh-six to Oh-ten."

"Oh-ten," Smith said, raising his eyebrows and blowing out a sigh, then standing with some difficulty from the little desk.

As Miss Schmulberg discreetly moved her hand to her Sig, unsnapping the strap, Carter Smith stretched out his aching back and rubbed at it. He said, "Well, Ms. Karen Schmulberg, that was all fascinating, I assure you. But I'm afraid the law's the law, and we're going to have to remove all these weapons. Today."

Karen Schmulberg was fast on the draw — *fastest in her class*. She aimed her Sig .40 at SAFE Agent Carter Smith's face and said, "I don't think so, Agent. You and your band of jack-booted thugs can just go back to that Washington swamp where you came from."

Smith chuckled. He'd heard it before — a thousand times at least by now — and he said, "Not without the guns, ma'am. Including that one."

He took one step forward, and Karen Schmulberg shot

him in the face.

Outside Ruger S. Sauer Elementary School, Smith's SAFE team, who had all been listening on their earbuds, heard his body hit the floor.

One of them said, "Carter?" When Smith did not respond, another said, "Plan B. Go!"

With that, all the agents moved forthwith to their SUVs and climbed in, spinning donuts around each other in the small parking area, causing the tank commanders and their teams to spin their cannons like drunken swordfighters until they clanked into each other and momentarily got wedged.

It appeared that the agents would make a clean getaway until grates opened and spike strips jabbed up, popping every tire that hit them and stopping them dead.

Knowing what was likely coming next, the agents dove from the SUVs with their dogs as Tank #1 freed his muzzle and fired a round, blowing the first SAFE car fifty feet in the air. It fell to the ground aflame as agents scurried for cover — there was none — while calling for backup.

Heavy backup.

Having a good sense of what they might be dealing with, the SAFE agents had come well-prepared — even more than usual. The night before, they had silently placed modern assault vehicles behind several houses around Ruger S. Sauer Elementary school — one of them inside a garage, from which it now exploded, and charged for the school walls with other assault vehicles, and *real* tanks, modern weapons of war not purchased from third-tier banana republics after being put out to pasture when no more Chinese parts were available. No, these were the latest American technology, including an M1A2/SEP Abrams and *two* MS Bradleys.

First, they blew up the elementary school tanks with wired

tank-busters. Then they did the same to all four guard towers, then the entire hardened "single entrance" front door. Then they blew holes in the hardened walls and drove through into Ruger S. Sauer Elementary School.

Karen Schmulberg heard the explosions and slapped the bolt back on her AR, but she did not get an opportunity to fire. An M9 Armored Earth Mover — which did not need firepower to get through the concrete walls — drove into her classroom and over her before she could get a single shot off, squishing her like an unwanted spider beneath a muddy combat boot.

Brave Colonel Darwin was next, running down the hall, waving his arms, yelling, "Surrender! I surrender! Don't shoot!" just before the Abrams fired. His pulpy remains coated the far security wall like a red Pollock.

In less than a minute, the enormous machines had crisscrossed the floorplan, and the roofs had collapsed in on them as they continued back out, unscathed.

Just before that, seconds after the inciting shot fired by *that crazy Schmulberg bitch*, Mr. Jenkins, Three-Jay as his friends and family called him, had run out the secret backdoor that only he and one other person knew about — that being Colonel Jonah T. Darwin, who did not make it.

Jenkins did not stop running until he was in his house, twenty-seven blocks away, with the doors locked, the curtains drawn, and his wife in his arms.

She said, "I told you those crazy-assed white folks were nothing but trouble."

Three-Jay agreed with her, as he always did, and resolved to try and get his old job back at the citrus processing plant down on Krome Avenue.

Most of the other school guards had the good sense — and lack of fealty — to lay down their weapons and were spared.

No charges were brought against them, but their guns were taken away, and they were debriefed. Basically, it went like this:

"Touch another gun, ever, and you're looking at life in Leavenworth."

In some ways, the raid was a success—Ruger S. Sauer Elementary School, K-6, was no more—but at a cost. Two ex-marines were dead, one of them a good man—though you never would have known it if you got the story from Frank and Eva on their designer couch.

Eva said, "Their precious rights and freedoms gone in sixty seconds."

"So fast," Frank said.

"Too fast," Eva said.

"So furious," Frank said.

"So am I," Eva said, though she did not appear to be. Probably the botox.

But Frank went positively lugubrious. "A sad day for education, Eva."

"A sadder day for America, Frank," Eva said.

In a bar at the Four Corners crossroads in the high country of Colorado, another television set was shot and sparking. This time it was Joline herself who had done the appliance assassinating. She turned up the country twang, drew herself a tall cold one—her earliest yet—and wondered what in the *hell* had happened to her nation and what would happen next.

She was to be mightily surprised.

Chapter Twenty

In the secret basement of the federal building that was still under indefinite repair, Harris Ball was at the desk he seemed never to leave—even though he felt remiss if he did not report that he had taken a "damned good shit" at least once a day, wherever it was, he went for that event. After said declaration, without putting down his beloved *WSJ* Business Section, Ball asked Mike Cho where they were at, timeline-wise.

Cho said, "I'd say we're over the hump, sir. Things are calming down. Operation Fierce Freedom is wrapping up—at least the initial phase. People are relaxing for the most part, with a few hot spots left, but the SAFE teams are hard at work."

A waft of sarcasm drifted through the room.

Ball grunted, set down his paper, picked up his cigar next to the No Smoking placard, and asked Cho how many guns were left to retrieve in America.

"Estimates are fifty, sixty million. It's hard to pinpoint, of course—there are pockets of activity, no doubt—but it looks like GCA has been quite successful."

Ball said, "Bad about Carter Smith. We served together in the Sand Pit back in Oh-twelve. Good man. Hated to see him cut down like that."

"Yes, sir. I'd heard good things about him," Cho said without any accompanying emotion.

Ball asked rhetorically, "Everyone's on their way?"

"If not en route, in preparation to become en route."

"Permits pulled."

"Pulled and certified."

"We're on schedule."

"Locked and loaded, you might say, sir."

"I wouldn't say that," Ball said. "Only a jackass would say that."

"Yes, sir. I am that jackass."

Ball closed his eyes and asked, "Why in Hell's good name, did I hire you again, Cho?"

"I brown-nose well, sir. Sixteen years of service in the military, never above the rank of corporal, third class."

"I thought you were a sergeant."

"No, sir. I bought these stripes after I got out. I like the way they look. Kind of like your posters back there."

Cho's *They almost look real* opinion not going unnoticed.

Ball said, "Jesus Christ," re: the fake stripes, spun his chair around to admire his *procured* "seals," then turned back with, "Get the hell outa here. And don't call me sir."

"Yes, sir," Cho said, and turned to leave.

"Wait!" Ball said. Cho stopped. Ball said, "Are we sure—I mean rock solid dead sure— that all the directives have been met and we are on schedule like a whore's period?"

"I believe so," Cho said. "Like I said, a few last pockets of resistance or just plain bad neighborhoods that SAFE teams haven't gotten to, but that's mainly due to their prioritization of high gun-density areas and soft targets."

"*Nice* neighborhoods," Ball said.

"They're saving the rotten ones for last—or they might ignore them altogether and just wait for the guns to show up in convenience store robberies and the like is what I'm hearing. Failed home invasions, liquor store stick-ups. That kind of thing."

"Stick-ups?" Ball said. "How old are you, Cho?"

"Thirty-four, sir. I'll be thirty-five in October."

"Happy birthday. Now get the fuck outa here. And let's shift to four daily briefings. Not that I want to see your ugly slant-eyed face every six hours, but I need to know what's going on as it happens."

Cho said, "I'll be more than happy to smell your stinking cigars and put up with your verbal harassment twice a day. Sir."

"Good. Dismissed, *Sergeant*."

Cho retreated, and Harris picked up his paper. The market had started to reinvigorate after the initial panic of GCA. Though the DOW had lost close to twenty percent in a remarkably short amount of time, a rebound was inevitable and had already begun. Once The Project was completed, Harris Ball expected a full recovery—because, he said under his breath, "It takes a nation of suckers and morons to make one man great."

Mike Cho had been correct in his assessments, based on data gathered by his SAFE sources. Operation Fierce Freedom was about to announce their success and plans to move to Phase II, in which most SAFE agents could go back to previous jobs at ATF, the FBI, the military, and other areas of law enforcement. Smaller teams would continue to look for single guns, but not too hard.

GCA had been mostly successful. But the results were, as before, varied.

In L.A., in Korea Town, shop owners still had the occasional well-hidden gun for defense against their black neighbors who would, they imagined, also still have guns, maintained for the sole reason—The Seoul reason, as they joked—of robbing them, though very few such events occurred.

Some educated and piss-poor folks in Appalachia and similar rural red regions across the country kept the family's heritage weapons for hunting food. Roadkill just was not a reliable source, especially in dry counties. And with the former administration having all but entirely gutted every social program developed over the previous hundred years to help them, they cussed the new president and polished the knobs on PawPaw's bolt-action varmint gun.

In suburban neighborhoods circling every major city in America, fathers who once kept multiple weapons in fancy gun safes—they called them "collections"—acceded to change and, after weeks of keeping their families locked up for safety reasons, started venturing out for paddle boating in the park, window shopping at the mall, and the simple joys of an ice cream cone without the fear of getting murdered or the need to strap to counter such a rare occurrence. Suddenly, they were happy to be relieved of the pressure of being the only good guy with a gun. Now they could just enjoy family time without the worry of assassination, assault, or retaliation, and they found, surprisingly—to them—that they liked it.

Deep in the Ozarks, one of the last SAFE teams followed up on a tip and raided a modern-day—to use the term loosely—commune. Agents had been tipped that the *communists* had a secret and terrifyingly large stash of attack weaponry. The lead likely came from a competing commune—really, a last compound—of heavily-armed preppers who had had all *their* terrifyingly large stash of attack weaponry seized the month

before. Or maybe it was just some snowflake-hating locals out
for some quick and easy domestic revenge.

Fundamentalist ratters-out.

When agents surprised the thirty-or-so hippies with a
pre-dawn raid, they were met by sleepy-eyed longhairs who
were unarmed in more ways than one. Not a single gun was
found. But when the groggy young folks saw the dogs, they
immediately confessed to having a large field of pot in the
hills and several kilos of just harvested weed drying in the
old tobacco barn. Agents explained to the kids that they were
not authorized to act on any crimes they discovered outside
their gun purview and shared a bong before leaving — after
advising the cord-cutters that though abortion carried the
death penalty in Missouri, smoking dope was now entirely
legal. Even growing it.

Missourians had their heads bolted on straight when it
came to priorities.

Everyone was ready for a break, but none more than the
meth-heads. Similar paranoias over unannounced agent raids
had spread throughout the "ice-skating" community — as well
as the ICE community — that SAFE agents could bust anyone
for anything they happened on that was illegal. Especially
meth, the biggest myth.

And the most dangerous.

The rumor spread like fire in a plastic-lined single-wide
cook lab with a gas stove pilot left on when multiple arrests
came pursuant to SAFE raids — weeks later. But that part of
the rapidly evolving lore did not make the rounds through
the always-reliable crystal grapevine.

The truth was that SAFE had happened on two large
warehouse-sized operations, one in Chicago and one outside
Las Vegas. When agents came for the weapons they knew

were in abundance, firefights broke out in both locations, and several members of the dealers' security details were killed.

The agents could not legally arrest anyone for cooking or dealing, so they did the next best thing: burned both buildings to the ground, citing "an unanticipated open flame" — after locating and confiscating all ledgers, routing/distribution details, and cell phones, all of which got turned over to DEA. *Then* the multiple arrests happened. As the meth community is wont to do, panic set in and mistakes were made, more arrests followed, and crime-fighters on the frontline of the latest war on dope rejoiced.

In smaller, rural cases — micro-labs in remote cabins and mobile RVs — SAFE agents found few or no guns, but they did discover children living in the back bedrooms while Mommy and Daddy cooked in the front. Since the duct-taped plastic draping tended to melt and drip in the not-uncommon lab fires, and kids often ended up in ERs with third-degree burns, SAFE agents similarly turned over the cooker-parents to local or DEA, often waiting on site until the transfer was complete and social services had the kids safely in custody. No one liked separating families, but in these cases, no one generally protested — not even the parents.

This kind of reasoning did not resonate with hardened addicts, especially in urban jungles, who spread the rumors like herpes in the nineties — and kept their guns, sometimes not even that well-hidden. SAFE agents were spread too thin to raid every suspected crack house and meth room in every major city, so the addicts were left to fend for themselves.

Omaha reported a not-uncommon event.

Three skeletal white meth-heads were smoking up in the back bedroom of an abandoned house when two other addicts burst in with guns, demanding the dope for their own use.

When one of the initial users pointed out that guns were illegal now and stood to protest the robbery, one of the interlopers shot him *and* his two buddies, and the thieves stole the dope. On their way outside, they stopped to make sure they had what they had come for via a quick snort when they heard footsteps behind them, realizing too late that they had not properly extinguished all three of their foes in the first volley and that remaining foe now held a 10-gauge pump shotgun. Unchoked, the big-bore Remington only took one pump, the resulting spray turning the two thieves into bug spray. Then the shotgun guy, ignoring his wound, tossed his gun aside and grabbed all the drugs for himself. In his estimation, the attempted robbery turned out well.

Then he overdosed.

SAFE got the guns, the city got the house, the coroner got the bodies—which no one claimed—and the cops got the blame. So, as Corporal "Sergeant" Cho had predicted, the situation took care of itself.

There were also the expected, if mostly benign, but occasionally tragic cases of if-only-I-still-had-my-gun situations, as happened in Compton where a divorced African American man heard banging at his door and reached for the gun he had always kept handy in the event of an attempted incursion into his personal domain and found it missing. He momentarily forgot that SAFE agents had done a thorough job in Compton, Watts, and Inglewood—South Central in general—and his gun was long gone. The pounding on his burglar bar door was followed with threats of "Open up, or we'll shoot!" "Give us your shit, or you're dead" and "Open the door, motherfucker, or we'll kill you, motherfucker!"

When quick but hearty attempts at pulling the door open failed, the man saw a stubby barrel appear between the bars and just made it out of the way of a burst of TEC-11 fire—almost. One of the bullets caught his calf, which he had not pulled fully behind his couch. When he cried out, one of his determined assailants felt that the next best move was to blow out the lock on the steel door. He racked his nine and shot at the heavy plate, catching it just above the deadbolt. The bullet ricocheted back and hit his homie in the chest. He went down, and the other two—shooter and accomplice—ran scared, leaving him behind to plead to the middle-aged divorcee, "Call 9-1-1, old man. I'm shot. I think I'm dyin'! Help me! Please!"

Though the homeowner had little sympathy for the wounded would-be thief at that moment, he made the call—mostly for himself—and both lived to tell the tale. He even declined to press charges and later took the young man in, giving him a job at his printing shop, saving a life.

If these stories were overloaded with irony, Brian Williams' last segment was wholly nuts, though the actual events were short-lived. As Williams reported:

"This morning, Canadian President Henri LeBlanc accused the United States of drawing his citizens into traps set by American U.S. Customs and Border Protection (CBP) agents to net rogue Canadians sneaking into the United States to 'aid their brethren.' Or as he put it, today…."

The screen went to video of LeBlanc shouting in French with captions that supported Williams' reporting. Though his message was unclear, Williams helped it make sense.

"As we first reported here last night, Canadian gun owners had been receiving coded messages from American ranchers just across the border in North Dakota, Montana, and Idaho, saying they desperately needed guns for protection against roving bands of modern-day cattle rustlers. As a result, sympathetic Canadian ranchers made the border crossings with hunting rifles and shotguns to aid their American counterparts. But, as reported today, the call for guns turned out to be a ruse when CBP officers were found to be waiting for the Canadians along with SAFE agents, who confiscated the Canadian guns and deported the Canadians back across the border. No one was arrested, but Prime Minister LeBlanc, a populist supporter of gun ownership in Canada, lodged a formal complaint with the White House, then went on air to vent about 'the illegal abandonment" of *our* Second Amendment.'"

Williams looked into the camera and again said, "You can't make this stuff up."

Although apparently, someone could – and did – as the entire story turned out to be faked by a group of dissident Canadian gun owners who made fake YouTube videos and sent them to LeBlanc, knowing he would fly off his French-Canadian handle and make waves. LeBlanc got punked. And he received no apology from American President Roger Pinkins. LeBlanc had the YouTubers arrested.

Williams wrapped up. "No word on when they may see the light of day. But the good news for them: their guns will be waiting."

Observers in countries all around the world had differing opinions as to what the fuck was going on in the United States. American credibility had been lost two presidents ago and had never recovered. Now, this.

"Les Americans sont plus fous que jamais!"

In Panama, in a well-guarded high-walled compound, former POTUS Ed Navarro watched the news with amusement, happy to be two-thousand miles from the madness inside the beltway. He and his wife drank rum and laughed at the fools so far away.

He said, "I never liked that guy."

His wife, Pauline, said, "Brian Williams?"

"Him either," Ed said.

"Oh, the French one," she said.

"French-Canadian," he said.

"I was never clear on the real difference," she said.

"Anger spectrum," he said.

And she said, "Either way, you got out just in time."

"Indeed, I did," he said happily. "Think I'll go for a swim."

"Enjoy yourself, dear," Pauline said. "Watch for sharks."

"I shall," he said, and gave her a peck.

Then ex-Prez Ed Navarro went for his daily swim in the warm, crystal clear waters of the Caribbean Sea, under the watchful eyes of a dozen secret service agents and their Panamanian counterparts, who never appeared fazed by Navarro's preference for dipping *au naturel* — as close as he or Pauline ever got to anything French.

Navarro had been a junior senator during the Freedom Fries and Toast non-revolution of the early aughts and still thought it to be one of the most embarrassing moments in recent history. At least now he and Pauline could laugh about it.

***

Up in the Colorado high country, the satellite TV connection went live, but David Billows was not watching it and not laughing. He was outside, wearing rubber boots, watching Carlos operating the track hoe, something the Nicaraguan American was very good at.

First, he dug a trench ten feet deep and thirty feet long, six feet deeper on the long end. Next, he drove back to the head of the ditch, where he carefully scraped out another foot of soil, exposing the lid of a large septic tank, which had a lifting hook in the middle. David wrapped a heavy chain around the track hoe bucket, climbed down into the hole, attached a hook at the other end of the chain to the eyehook in the center of the slab, and climbed back out.

Carlos raised the heavy slab out of the pit, swung it to one side clear of the hole, and gently set it down on the unturned earth. David freed the chain from the bucket and stepped back so that Carlos could lower the bucket back into the full septic tank and shove the far blocks into the long, deep ditch. Sewage flowed out thick and fast into the catch basin, revealing the bottom of the empty tank in less than a minute — another slab with another large eyehook in the center.

David hosed off the bucket and the slab, rewrapped the chain around the bucket, and climbed back down into the emptied tank, unconcerned with the detritus or odor, to attach the chain to the new hook. Carlos then delicately lifted the second slab straight up and out of the hole to reveal a dry chamber underneath, packed with hundreds of guns and tens of thousands of rounds of ammo.

Carlos grinned and said, "The Underground — protecting America for generations."

By now, everyone had come outside to watch and marvel. David gave the order to "Pack 'em up," and his crew went to work, even the kids.

Marjorie stayed back, coming over to put her arm around David's waist and lean her head on his shoulder. After a moment of watching the first bucketload of weapons come out of the hole to be loaded into the waiting empty Schwan's truck, she said, "Will you be coming back?"

He said, "Not likely." And she held him closer.

Two hours later, David and Carlos were on the road, the

latter driving. They would stay on 50 until it became 56, then I-35 at Emporia, up to 70, and across to 64. Pretty much a straight shot.

David had chosen a Schwan's truck for its under-ten-thousand-pound gross vehicle weight and no need for special DOT licenses, and Carlos had arranged for a GPS tracking device whose number was added to a national registry as compliant with all weight provisions so as not to have to stop at weigh stations. If they *were* pulled, each reefer door, when opened, revealed only frosty boxes with names like "Beef Pot Pies," "Red Baron Pizza," and "Rainbow Confetti Ice Cream." All carried the red Schwan's stylized swan label, noting the company was "Est.1952."

To make sure everything on the other end was as promised, David checked in one last time to verify that all systems were go. Using his first burner, he dialed a 202 area code number. When someone answered, he said, "It's Red Fox, put me through."

He was put on hold—computer music.

"'Billy Jean,' the elevator version," David said to Carlos. "Whole district of losers."

Carlos said, "No respect in the Beltway. I'm tellin' you when I worked for Senator Blackmon—"

David held up his finger for silence and said to the person on the other end of the line that he did not like being put on hold. "These calls can be traced, you know." The other party said something, and David replied, "Right, yeah. No one in the IC knows how to beat an encrypted signal. You obviously don't remember when that nine-year-old hacked the Pentagon." As the person on the other end made what might have been a comedic comment, David cut him off. "Thirty-six hours if we don't run into weather or other problems."

He then tossed the phone out the window into traffic.

CHAPTER TWENTY-ONE

In Washington, President Pinkins' chief of staff Henry Hillerman determined that it was time for another presidential address from the Oval Office, to let America know how well things were going.

With a few caveats.

After the usual hubbub, the space was cleared, those in attendance watched from the sidelines, and Roger Pinkins, POTUS, spoke to the American people.

"Fellow Americans, I come to you not solely as your president, but as a friend. I know many of you may not think of me as a friend, but I remind opponents of GCA of a few things. One, I was opposed to the law from the beginning. Other members in my party brought it to the floor in Congress and, due to their then and current 'ownership' of both houses, were able to pass the bill, which my predecessor Edward Navarro signed into law."

To allow a moment, Pinkins looked down as if to review his notes as Ed Navarro had done in his addresses, then returned to the teleprompter.

"Others of you don't care for me simply because of my party affiliation. I am a Democrat. I have been a Democrat all my political life, and I ran for president as a Democrat, accepting my party's nomination last July. As you may recall, I won handily in November with 328 Electoral College votes and fifty-three percent of the popular vote. My opponent received only 210 Electoral College votes and less than forty-seven percent of the popular vote. I say this to remind you all that I was duly elected as your president, both by the Electoral College and the popular vote. Further, I accepted the outcome of that election with the promise to work squarely with both sides of the aisle, as I said many times."

"Squarely on both sides" was a silly campaign slogan that had worked beyond anyone's highest expectations, so Pinkins took every opportunity to replay it.

He went on. "In the spirit of bipartisanship, I agreed to make no effort to repeal or in any way undermine GCA and its consequences for America, as dubious as I was about taking away Americans' right to own arms under the Second Amendment. But I have several confessions to make."

He paused for effect, this time not looking away.

"First, I think we have all been surprised by the efficacy of the SAFE Administration's actions. In just over nine weeks, these faithful defenders of American law and freedom have removed close to ninety-five percent of all handguns, long rifles, and assault weapons — from legitimate gun owners, to collectors, to criminals. I have been assured that by the end of the year, we will be at ninety-nine-point-seven percent *recoverage*. For many, this is worrisome. But for others, a blessing."

Pinkins had balked at the use of "recoverage," but his speechwriter won out and, once he used the newly minted word, the president felt fine having said it, as the word cleverly conveyed the concept.

He continued. "This leads me to confession Number Two.

I have, somewhat surprisingly, found myself in the latter group. I am relieved. I did not think I would say this, make a public statement of relief and satisfaction over the removal of all guns from the American tapestry, but I am, and I have. And I do not stand alone. We have commissioned extensive polling, some of which I am sure you have seen, as to our fellow Americans' responses and feelings in the aftermath of this monumental change to the nation's lifestyle. As of this morning, we have reason to believe that an overwhelming majority of voters agree: GCA is a resounding success. The National Mall is open for business again!"

Barricades had been taken down, and tourists were welcome back.

"Not only that," Pinkins said, "but confidence in the federal government is the highest it's been in seventy-five years." He smiled. "We did something right for once. We passed a mostly unpopular law, saw it through — via aggressive enforcement — and have reaped the early results. Over sixty-seven percent of Americans say they are pleased with the results of GCA. They feel safer in their hometowns and cities. And they are confident that this era of peace will continue and bring lasting effects to America — *positive* effects. But most importantly, they Do. Not. Miss. Their. Guns."

Pinkins let that sink in while staring into the camera, then said, "Confession Number Three: I am surprised, delighted, and happy I was wrong." His final breather, then, "We are a safer country for GCA. It took us countless blood-soaked decades to catch up with the rest of the modern world, but by the grace of God, we have done it — even surpassed it. We are firmly ensconced in the 21st century, along with our peaceful international friends around the world. We are finally an integral part of modern global life. And we are *all* better for it.

The numbers prove it. We are nearly gun-free and happier for it because we are also gun-*death* free."

He grinned confidently.

What POTUS left out was that rates of death by guns had soared over those nine weeks but were mostly the result of diehards—literally—who refused to give up their guns, choosing Suicide by SAFE, as it came to be known. The upside, which Pinkins also did not mention, was that in this swell of fatalities, many of the nation's hardcore lunatics, who had been armed to the teeth, were gone. America *was* safer. Especially from domestic terrorism.

POTUS ended with, "Death from guns, from crimes committed by civilians in the last two weeks, is the lowest ever recorded in recent American history. That is something to be celebrated, friends. We are safer, we are alive, and we will remain both safer and alive, thanks to GCA."

The final-final pause.

"So I say thank you to all my fellow Americans who willfully participated in the Gun Care Act—especially those who did so reluctantly. We are better for it, and you, my fellow Americans, have earned my greatest respect. Good day and God bless."

Roger Pinkins smiled, the cameras were turned off, the teleprompters went dark—and the phones started ringing off the hook. Most calls were positive. Some folks were still angry—epithets were recorded, and secret service agents would be making visits here and there—but for the most part, roughly seventy percent, Americans pledged peace and swore allegiance to a gun-free America. Operation Fierce Freedom had, against all odds, and a terrible moniker, worked perfectly.

CHAPTER TWENTY-TWO

The president's speech was timely, as planned by Henry Hillerman, to precede the March for Guns planned for the next day in D.C. when perhaps hundreds of thousands of disgruntled former gun owners would show their dismay over and disgust with the new law — the other thirty percent — now that D.C. was again open to the public, though great uncertainty remained regarding the wisdom of that timing. But the president had promised, weeks ago, and he was a man who honored his own words with action.

Still, speeches were planned at several points along the march route up Constitution and over to Pennsylvania, ending up back at The Mall where a Ted Nugent memorial band concert was the main "entertainment."

Counter-protests were also planned by Tupac's kids, along with Columbine, Sandy Hook, Parkland, and other survivors of gun violence and its ancillary traumas. Most were expected to be peaceful, but no one was letting their guard down. All active-duty cops and park rangers, SWAT teams, and National Guard "preparedness teams" were called to serve for the weekend.

Security would remain tight until the protests were over, and SAFE teams could round up those last pesky twenty-million guns. Cal Worthing said it best at one of his daily briefings to the White House Press Corps. "Who would have thought that twenty-million guns was a drop in the bucket?" When asked if Operation Fierce Freedom was close to closing its doors, Worthing said, "I have not spoken to the president about that." When pushed by another reporter on the same topic, Worthing said, "Look, I think we can all see the end of the rainbow, and that pot of gold—free and easy access for all Americans to the living freedom they so dearly hold—at the grand finale." Several reporters squinted, unsure of what Worthing meant. He said, "The end is near, I'm sure," and left the room.

What he did not tell the press corps, and what he had hoped like hell they would not ask because he further hoped that they had not heard anything about it, was that Carl "Tommy" Cuatrel of naked trailer fame had sent a letter to President Pinkings [sic] saying that he wanted to apologize for his "bad behavior."

In person.

For a reason neither Cal Worthing nor Roger Pinkins could understand, a meeting was arranged—at a Sizzler Steakhouse away from the city. Pinkins did not even know there were any still open.

"Why am I meeting this idiot again? And why in a Sizzler?"

"It's what he wanted," Vice President Sally Hawkins told him.

Pinkins looked to his CoS Hillerman, who shrugged.

"Jesus," Pinkins said. "He couldn't come here? I mean, it is the fucking White House."

"Well, he could," Sally hedged. "But then you'd have that nut in the Oval Office. Press corps would be on full alert, and if anything bizarre happened — "

Hillerman said, "Oh, what could possibly go wrong with a dummie-hanging racist lunatic wandering around these hallowed halls with a president he openly slandered?"

"Exactly," Sally said.

Pinkins put his face in his hands and rubbed his temples. He had been doing that a lot in the past ten weeks. He said to his desk, "No press?"

"No press," Hillerman said.

"Also what he wanted," Sally said.

Pinkins looked up. "Why?" The underlying question being: *Why wouldn't a lunatic like that want all the press he could summon up?*

"As I understand it," Hillerman said, "he was happy coming to the White House, but secret service talked him out of it."

"Security concerns," Sally Hawkins said.

"Press concerns," Hillerman said. "Much more important." Happy that he got a rare chuckle out of his boss, Henry added, "I'm told we're making sure there won't be a reporter or a cellphone for ten blocks in any direction."

Pinkins weighed the concept a moment, then said, "I suppose if I must meet with this nutbag, I might as well do it in secret. Just in case it goes off the rails."

Sally said, "That would be my choice."

Hillerman said, "And if nothing bizarre happens, we can issue a press release and spin it however we want. 'Blithering racist comes to his senses' type of thing."

Pinkins grunted, then asked if Sally was going.

She laughed and said, "No. I think you can handle this one on your own, Roger. Besides, I've got a tipping-point meet with Speaker Cornwall to bend his ear about allowing a clemency bill for GCA offenders to come to the floor."

"I like that idea," Pinkins said.

Hillerman did too. "Might help our numbers edge up a bit more."

Though the majority of Americans were pleased with the outcome of GCA, POTUS's numbers kept hovering in the mid-forties—up from twenty-eight just weeks before. The White House press machine had been steadily beating the drum of Pinkins' lack of involvement and opposition to GCA.

Then he changed his mind, made his speech, and nothing exploded.

POTUS asked, "When is this historic meeting with my personal weirdo supposed to happen?"

"Tomorrow at noon," Hillerman said. He turned to the vice president. "That's right, isn't it? I wasn't clear whether it was tomorrow or Sunday."

"Tomorrow," she said.

Pinkins pointed out, "During the rally? The protest?"

"Perfect time to have some privacy," she said. "Everyone else will be otherwise occupied. And you will be clear of any fracases."

"I suppose that's true," Pinkins allowed. And again, "If anyone had told me...."

He shook his head.

***

That night, Roger Pinkins shared a late dinner with his wife, the former Lorelei "Daisy" Manors, in their quarters. Being their 29th anniversary *and* her birthday, he did it up right—had the White House chef make her favorite, lobster bisque with Ritz crackers, and bring it up on a cart.

"Room service for the birthday girl," the chef joked after knocking on the main door. He had the most casual relationship with the first couple of anyone on staff because he had known them the longest, over twenty-five years.

A nice Pahlmeyer chardonnay accompanied the meal of tiny-greens salad, fresh buttered asparagus, and sea bass with a horseradish and sriracha honey-glaze — they liked the kick — followed by blueberry sorbet topped with white sprinkles.

The Pinkins's had eclectic tastes.

After watching a rerun of *House of Cards* — laughing all the way through at how tame the show now seemed — they tucked in for some anniversary sex and a glass of port, nary a word spoken about this nutty meeting with crazy Carl "Tommy" Cuatrel from Ocklawaha, Florida. However, an approaching battle with Congress over allowing the purchase of contraceptives for teenagers over the age of fourteen, without their parents' knowledge, kept POTUS awake until three. He was up at six, though, as always, and in the gym doing his usual rigorous routine. Today was arms and back, followed by thirty on the elliptical. Then a steam, a cold shower, a shave, and dress for success. He favored expression of such with a Hugo Boss suit and tie, midnight blue today.

After the regular morning security briefing from his DNI and CIA chiefs, Pinkins had a sparse breakfast — "Gotta leave room for the salad bar," he joked — then watched live coverage of the protests taking shape around the city. Turnout was less than expected, but still, close to a hundred thousand angry former gun nuts showed up to piss and whine. Confrontations were few and brief, fortunately. By late morning, only one woman had been knocked to the ground by a bearded vet with a tattoo that read, "Freedom is for ALL!"

Just apparently not for her.

At eleven-thirty, Pinkins' press secretary Cal Worthing came in with CoS Henry Hillerman to say the cavalcade was ready and parked out back.

Pinkins said, "Are we really doing this?"

"It appears we are," Hillerman said, almost giddy.

Pinkins sighed and asked Worthing what he thought about the whole Cuatrel affair. Cal said, "I'm sorry secret service decided not to have the press there. I think it would be a terrific opportunity to show that you mean what you said about burying the hatchet, partisanship-wise."

"I'd like to bury it in Sally Hawkins forehead for concocting this whole mess," Henry said.

"I thought it was the Office of Public Engagement," Pinkins said.

"Well, them too," Worthing said. "They suggested it in the first place, I think."

"I've never even seen his letter," Pinkins said, referring to Cuatrel's initial contact.

"I think it was an email," Hillerman said.

Worthing joked, "Sent from his brand-new iPhone 15Xi from his single-wide in Bumfuck Nowhere, Florida."

They all got a chuckle from the relevant irreverence, and Worthing said, "Shall we?"

"You're going?" Pinkins said. "Please tell me you're going."

"No, sir. I have a briefing in the press room at noon—on the protests and all."

"Anything horrible to report?"

"Not yet."

"Well, there's that."

And they headed downstairs.

The rear portico was teeming with secret service, though they seemed to be keeping a lower than usual profile, probably to avoid the appearance to reporters outside that anything unusual or secret or nefarious or whatever-the-fuck snoopy reporters imagined was going on behind closed doors was now coming outside. As far as anyone could tell, Pinkins and Henry Hillerman slipped into the second limo, between the two decoy limos, without being seen.

Pinkins looked surprised. "Oh. Are you coming along, Henry?" he said.

"I had a clear schedule," Henry said. "And since you seemed a little on edge about this...." He paused. "I can stay behind if you prefer."

"No, no, please!" Pinkins said. "I'm happy for a friendly face on this ludicrous adventure."

"It's going to be an adventure, all right," Henry said, chuckling. "Have you read the file on this guy?" Pinkins said he had not, so Hillerman handed it over.

Pinkins glanced over it as the procession started away. "Jesus," he said. "This guy's all over the place."

The file contained photos of Cuatrel's trailer over the years. Apparently, he had become a local "favorite," with lots of people taking lots of pictures and sending them to the Belleview paper, which, on occasion, published one if it was outlandish enough. Over the years, Cuatrel had put up various large signs protesting Catholicism, Hedonism (the resort), mixed marriage, gay marriage (of course), and veganism (saying it was "Satan's digestive pathway to hell").

He once protested the existence of starfish. They regenerate! his signs read.

On the flip side, he also had issues — according to the signs — with former Republican House Speaker Dalton Dithers, Libertarian candidate for the presidency, feminist Allison Calmers, and Independent state senator Sheila E. Rothstein. The last one had yellow six-pointed stars around the words, Give Gaza Back to the Towelheads.

His messages were not always clear—which was what made him a local favorite.

Pinkins said, "I suppose, on seeing all this, he would seem to be—"

"Thoroughly confused?" Henry Hillerman said.

"I was going to say harmless."

"My guess."

Pinkins glanced over another page, Cuatrel's service record. "Says he did three tours in Viet Nam."

"No wonder he's crazy," Henry said.

"Earned two Bronze Stars," Pinkins said, flipping the page. "Owned a television repair store."

Hillerman said, "*Before* he went to Nam?"

Pinkins chuckled. "And a poultry farm...." He flipped another page. "And a palm reading booth that he traveled around the state with...." And finally, "Oh my god." Pinkins looked up.

"You saw that, huh?"

"A porn actor? Really? *That* guy?"

"Each to her own."

"Lordy," Pinkins said. "I hope there are no tapes."

As the president's motorcade slid past the concrete barriers that had been placed for six blocks around the Sizzler, Pinkins grimaced. "Was all this really necessary?"

A secret service agent in front said, "For your safety, sir."

Pinkins said, "What if a regular paying customer needs a steak fix?"

"They'll have to wait until after one, sir."

Pinkins lowered his voice to Hillerman. "I swear these people are inventing ways to make me less popular than I already am, and I haven't been at this three months."

"Now you know how Obama felt," Hillerman said.

Pinkins said, "How was it working for him? You've never really spoken about it."

"A little more fun than working for you, sir," Hillerman said honestly. "He's got a terrific sense of humor."

Pinkins scowled slightly; he knew he was not known for his comedic fluency. But then, he had had to deal with this goddamned GCA bullshit from day one.

"On the other hand," Hillerman said, "a lot fewer death threats — at least racist ones."

Pinkins was not certain that was a compliment or not. But it was true — nearly one-hundred-percent of *his* death threats were over his following the goddamned law, not being African American.

"Fucking guns," he said. "You see, Henry? It's good they're gone. Never did anyone any real good. I've come around on that."

"So you said in your address, sir."

"Well, goddammit, I mean it. I was wrong. I was just fucking wrong."

"We're all wrong from time to time, sir. Even presidents."

"Especially presidents — naming no names," Pinkins said, and made Henry laugh again.

POTUS's motorcade filled up most of the parking lot at the suburban Sizzler. While agents ran around in all directions, confirming that all was secure — they had already put their men and women inside and out — the president and his chief of staff looked out the limo windows at the standard controlled chaos and let their own thoughts roam.

Pinkins was not sure what Henry was thinking, but *he* was wondering how many more ridiculous meetings like this he would have to endure over the next four years. He had already decided not to run again. Once was enough.

The door opened, and the president's lead agent said, "All clear, sir. If you'll come with me." Then he told Hillerman, "You can remain in the car if you like, sir."

"No, I think I'll come in," Hillerman said. "I wouldn't miss this for the world." He got out, grinning from ear to ear, mainly just to annoy his boss.

The lead agent said, "Your choice, sir," and led the way, making sure that all his people were in place—the right place—and that his pre-placed snipers had a clean line from their triangulated positions on rooftops around the lot.

Inside, the Sizzler was mostly empty.

"Where is everyone?" Pinkins asked.

An agent just inside the door said, "We sent everyone home except key personnel."

"Great," Pinkins said. "Now they can all be pissed at me for missing work, too."

Henry made a note and said, "I'll make sure they get paid for today, sir. And we'll send fruit baskets."

"Good," Pinkins said, looking around and spotting the lone, grey, balding white man sitting in a booth by himself, faced away. "Is that him?" Pinkins asked.

The inside agent said, "Yes, sir. That's Mr. Cuatrel. He's expecting you."

Pinkins looked to see if the woman was joking and was disappointed to find that apparently, she was not. But then she didn't look like the type to enjoy a joke—kind of like his lead agent, who had stayed outside and was chattering away into his sleeve like a teenager yacking about who was selling pot this week during recess and got suspended.

Pinkins shook his head, certain that he would never get used to this job even if he did hold office for eight years.

If anyone had told him....

"Mr. Cuatrel," Pinkins said, putting on his best neutral campaign smile.

"Yes, sir!" Cuatrel said, standing too quickly and knocking over his water. "Aw, shit. Try to make a good impression...."

A waiter wearing a white apron and a disapproving scowl came over to wipe up the water, managing to flip some onto the front of Cuatrel's khaki trousers. "Sorry, sir," he said, and retreated.

Cuatrel looked down. "Crap. Looks like I pissed myself in front of the president. I hope there ain't any cameras out there."

"There aren't, I assure you," Pinkins said, extending his hand. "It's...interesting to meet you, Mr. Cuatrel."

"Ha!" Cuatrel said, appreciating the joke more than the SS woman—another *Ilsa*, this one more of a Helga—and he shook the president's hand enthusiastically.

"Sit, please," Pinkins said, after retrieving his blood-starved fingers, and sat into the opposite side of the booth. He looked across and said, "So...."

CHAPTER TWENTY-THREE

Downtown, a Schwan's truck with Colorado plates was waved past a unit of National Guardsmen, around a barrier, and into the underground parking garage of a particular unoccupied federal building that was perpetually under repair.

Never-a-sergeant Mike Cho met "patriot outlaw" David Billows and his man Carlos on the loading dock as Carlos unlocked the many side doors on the rear reefer, and Cho's crew removed frosty fake box covers to reveal the massive load of weapons.

"Wow," Cho said. "You really delivered."

"Fifteen semi tractor trailers on the way," David said without emotion. "They have to be more careful and will take a few more hours."

"I'm impressed," Cho said. "I had my doubts."

David Billows said, "You don't even know me." Something in the way he said it shut Mike Cho up. David said to him, "Let's get this over with. I'm not much for cities."

"Sure," Cho said. "Semper Fi, man. This way." When Carlos started to go with them, Cho told him, "Whoa, dude. Just him. You're not on the guest list."

David said to his partner, "It's cool, CJ. We'll catch up."

"Right on," Carlos said, and turned to one of the camo'd helpers. "These going to the rally?"

"Yeah, buddy," the guy said in a Louisiana drawl. "Should make it a speck more interesting."

"I'd say," Carlos said, watching his friend being swallowed into the building.

A three-minute walk and two body searches later— "No weapons allowed down here," Cho told him—and David Billows was in Harris Ball's "office." David looked up at the faux shields behind Ball and said, "Nice shields. What do they mean?"

"They mean," Ball said, craning back to look and admire the work he'd had commissioned, "We won."

David nodded as if that meant something and moved ahead with business. "Is this going to take long?"

"No longer than you make it," Ball said, lighting a new ever-present cigar. He did not offer one to David. He said, "So, tell me, Pillows—"

"Billows. With a B," David said.

"Billows, right," Ball said. "Weird name."

"Yeah, not as pun-worthy as yours," David said. "Or is that an anagram? I always get them confused. Maybe a Spoonerism. Are you up on your Monty Python?"

"No," Ball said flatly, and shoved his *WSJ* aside. "So, you have a dozen semis loaded and ready."

"Fifteen, and they're on the road now. They should reach their assigned destinations by the end of the day."

Harris Ball perked up. "Excellent! Now, we're talking. You might just get your own territory outa this." He dangled it out there like it meant something.

David ignored it like it did not. "So, what's next?"

"I don't normally discuss that," Ball said. "Top secret shit, you know. But since we're amongst friends." He looked over to Cho. "Mike, tell him."

Cho grinned wide and said, "We take over."

"Take over what?" David said.

"Everything," Cho said matter-of-factly.

"What are you going to do with 'everything'?"

"Whatever we want," Cho said. "Right, boss?"

"Bingo-dingo."

David did his best to pretend not to be bothered by any of this silliness. He said, "What is 'everything'?"

"Everything is everything," Ball said. "Whole country."

David acted impressed. "The whole country."

"All of it," Ball said. "We staged a revolution — a successful silent coup if you will — and we get it all as a reward."

"All."

"Everything," Ball said, beaming, and puffed away.

David nodded passively and said, "I heard you had big plans, but...."

"Huge," Mike Cho said. "And you'd be amazed who all is involved."

Ball said, "Michael, you can either a) shut up now, or b) leave."

Cho chose shutting up.

David said to Ball, "But you've got help."

"Oh yeah," Harris said. "Plenty of it. We're just the tip."

David said, "I don't know if I'd use that particular term these days."

"Yeah, funny guy," Ball said. But he was in too good a mood to quibble. "We are the spearhead, if you prefer. We made the whole damn thing happen. All the guns are gone, except for the ones we have, the ones you're bringing us, and a few in the hands of criminals we can easily control."

"Probably already work for you," David said.

"Probably," Ball allowed without dissent. "They're not as important as the mainstage players we have in place."

David nodded as if interested, and said, "So the country is yours."

"One-hunnert percent," Ball said, trying his hand at black comedian impression gold. What he thought it would sound like, Ball being terminally white.

"Okay," David said. "And, if I may, what do you plan to do with it? Now that you 'own' it."

"Make money, Billows," Ball said. "Lots and lots and lots of beautiful, green, gorgeous *money*."

"I see," David said.

Ball told him, "Play your cards right, and you could end up with a trillion or two yourself," and laughed at his *mild* exaggeration.

David said, humbly, "I'm more of a few-hundred-thousand guy. My needs are simple."

Ball cocked his head. "Each to his own. You like it out there in the sticks?"

"Wouldn't live anywhere else," David said. "But you...I recognize you. You're already kind of rich, right? Investments or something. Real estate. What do you need more for?"

Ball stood and held his hands out like Brazil Jesus. "For my flock." He grinned wide.

"And they are?"

"These fine men and women down here, working their asses off in this hellish basement for six months. My wife and kids. Their kids. Every loyal patriot and hardworking corporation in America. The caviar of the elite. Everyone wins because *we* won. What we had before was peanuts. This is the whole enchilada. We worked for it, and it's ours."

Though David had an opinion about Ball's buffet of mixed metaphors, he said nothing.

Ball stepped around his desk to continue. "We won because we were smarter, better prepared, had bigger balls, knew what we wanted and how to get it, and went after it, and got it. We. Fucking. Won. America is ours, now, Billows. All ours. We own the United States of Fucking America!"

"The money," David said, as an assumption.

Ball took as many strutting steps as space would allow and said, "Are you kidding me? Money? That's only part of it. We own it *all*, man—all of it. Hell, we *are* it from now on. It is us. We are it. We *are* the United Fucking States of Fucking America!"

David was thinking that Harris Ball was a tad over-the-top carried away with his own sense of grandeur, but shaking his head as if impressed, said, "Wow. I gotta give it to you. Like Sergeant Cho said here—"

"He's not a real sergeant," Ball said.

David said, "Right," as if he already knew that and plowed ahead—or perhaps did not and didn't care, as if Cho was a nobody regardless of what rank he bestowed upon himself. "Like he said, I had my doubts. But I did what was asked of me, and I delivered."

"You sure did, boy!" Harris balled.

"And, well...," David said, as if awestruck, wondering if now he was too over-the-top and Ball might not trust his sincerity. He laid it on even thicker. "You did it," David said. "You pulled it off. Fucking amazing. Like I said: Wow. Just... *wow.*"

He threw the first smile he had shown anyone in months— the time just had not been right—and held out his arms. Not Brazil Jesus, but loving, admiring, secular Jesus.

He wanted a hug.

Ball laughed, filled with his sense of self-worth and evil accomplishment, held open his hands, and stepped forward.

In a flash, David was behind him, with Ball's head in a military-strength chokehold.

Former corporal Cho lost his shit. "What…what the fuck are you doing, man?! That's the fucking president! You can't do that! Let him go!"

David did not let go, despite burly Ball's best efforts to free himself while shouting, "You fucking cocksucker! I'll have you drawn and quartered and served to my fucking pigs!"

"Not gonna happen, Harry," David said calmly.

Cho was severely flummoxed. "He's the *president*!"

"Of what?" David said. "The loony farm?"

Ball shouted, "I'll have you executed for treason, you sonofabitch!"

"No, you won't. And you know why, Harry?" David said, as calmly as if ordering an extra pickle at his favorite New York deli. "You're not leaving this room. Ever."

"Fuck you! You're dead!" Ball screamed. Then, as if just realizing it, he yelled at Cho, "And what the fuck are you going?! Help me! Kill him!"

"With what?" Cho said. "There are no guns!"

"Use your fucking hands! A stapler! A goddam pencil, I don't care! Just kill him!"

Cho had no idea what to do and was clearly afraid of what David might do to him, so he chose yelling, "Help! We need some assistance in here! Stat! Help!"

Though the arm around Ball's neck made it difficult to move, his jaw dropped. He said, "You fucking moron. How *did* you get this job?" Then he yelled again, "KILL HIM

NOW!" and struggled to no avail. "Use your karate or some fucking shit!"

Cho ignored the stereotype and took an uncertain step forward, clearly out of confusion and a sense of misplaced duty. To which David said, "One more step, Michael, and I will snap his neck like a cockroach's leg."

Cho no doubt saw the fragility of a cockroach's leg in his mind's eye and stopped.

"You fucking kill him, or I'll kill *you!*" Ball threatened his aide, having mostly given up on thrashing as it had not done any good. And he no doubt had the same roach's leg image in his mind—just above his neck. "For treason!" Ball yelled Cho.

Now, Cho was genuinely conflicted.

David said, "Let me make this easier for you, Michael."

And David Billows snapped Harris Ball's neck with no more effort than breaking that imagined roach's spindly leg. Ball dropped to the floor like a bloated sack of rotten potatoes.

Kind of like what he was.

Cho stared. "Why...did you do that? All of our plans...."

All. Gone.

"Because, Corporal Cho, Harris Ball represents all I fought against in *my* three tours. Everything America said it was and had been for 250 years. Everything that somehow got lost along the way in the last few decades—that rotted and smelled and brought disgrace to this great country all over the world. Because we who invented Democracy all but killed it in the name of profits and greed. Your boss here, this sanctimonious piece of fascist shit, represented everything that was wrong with America and the world. I was sent to fix that problem." David Billows looked down at the result of his good work and said: "Consider it fixed." He looked up. "Any further questions or thoughts, Mike?"

Cho likely had a plethora of questions and thoughts, but not one dared make it to his lips.

David stepped over to the desk and picked up an official-looking booklet that could have been printed in the government printing office. He read the title, "Operation Fierce Freedom Rules of Engagement," then looked up. "Yeah?"

Cho said, "There were no rules."

"Exactly," David said.

"But...." Cho had no idea what to do. He was alone in the room with the next dead president-*elect* and the man who killed him.

That man said, "He set up that Safest School in America with his own money, didn't he?" Cho nodded. "We lost a good man in that clusterfuck. A fellow Marine named Carter C. Smith." David nodded down. "Ball's little psycho-bitch Karen Schmulberg shot him in the face — for no reason, other than believing in this ridiculous horseshit."

David Billows stepped behind Ball's desk and opened a drawer, saying, "So you see, Corporal Cho, we didn't need fewer guns...we needed fewer assholes." He reached into the desk and pulled out Ball's Colt .45 semi-auto, and said, "In here all along. I'll bet you didn't see that coming."

"We're...not allowed to have...guns in here," Cho spluttered, feeling helpless.

"Except the bossman," David said. "Always except the bossman. Some president, huh?" He looked over the desk at the dead fat man on the floor. "Won't be missed."

Two camo'd soldiers now ran in, having heard the commotion probably, and stopped short when they saw David holding a forbidden gun.

Brave Mike Cho yelled, "Get him!"

To dissuade that possibility, David reached over the desk

and shot the already dead Harris Ball in the head. Bits of bone and grey matter splattered onto the men's boots charged with "getting" David Billows.

They did not advance.

"Good choice, fellas," David said.

Mike Cho warned emptily, "You'll never get out of here alive."

David said, "Oh, I might," just as several large explosions were heard down the halls. He checked his watch. The time was precisely 12:15 p.m., as planned.

CHAPTER TWENTY-FOUR

Five minutes earlier, at 12:10 in the Sizzler Steakhouse, Carl "Tommy" Cuatrel had told President Roger J. Pinkins that it was "an honor" to meet him. To which President Pinkins had said, "Really. Because it didn't look like you felt that way before."

Cuatrel hung his head. "Yeah, the mannequins. That was a dumb thing to do. I'm sorry," he said sheepishly. "I'd like to make it up to you."

"That's fine, Mr. Cuatrel. No need."

"No, I insist," Carl said. "I came prepared. But first, you have to try this tuna salad. It is the best danged tuna salad I have ever tasted in my *life*. And my grandmammy could make some damn tuna salad, now."

Pinkins was game. "What was her secret?"

"Old South Sweets," Carl said. "The pickles? They got some whang, Buddy!" He nodded at his small plate with the large mound of tuna salad before him. "Now this, I must admit, is not Grandmammy good, but it's damn close. Different, it is. You have to try some."

"I will in a minute," Pinkins said.

"No, I insist. These boys told me that you would break bread with me and respect what I had to say."

Sounding both hurt and peeved, he nodded at the secret service people.

Pinkins looked over and caught Henry Hillerman biting his lip so hard it looked like it might bleed, his entire body jerking to contain his hysterics.

Pinkins had to laugh. "All right," he said. "Someone bring me a scoop."

He turned to the closest agent—the humorless woman from before, who did not appear inclined to be a waitress. She nodded to a man in a white serving apron. He nodded back and went to the salad bar, reached under the sneeze guard, dug out a healthy scoop of Sizzler Tuna Salad Supreme, plopped it on a saucer, and brought the plate to Agent Helga, who then set it on the table in front of President Pinkins, who said, "Thank you," and looked to see that blood was now trickling down Henry's lip.

Henry Hillerman was convulsing so hard he had to turn away.

As "Tommy" Cuatrel continued to savor each delectable bite of his chunk-light tuna salad—with a small amount of dribbling—he said, "You tell me that ain't the best damn tuna salad you've ever had outside your own family." Because, as he admitted, "We all have our family favorites. But outside that...." He took another bite and "Mmmmm"d. Then he said, "Really, Mr. President, this is just so nice of you, sir. I mean, after I was such an asshole and all."

The president remained gracious. "We all have our moments, I suppose, Mr. Cuatrel," he said, still unsure of why he had to meet with this dribbler in the first place, much less pretend to like tuna salad that been out on that salad bar counter for who knew how long.

Cuatrel shrugged off his previous actions. "I was pissed

about the guns."

"You weren't alone," Pinkins said.

"No sir, I know that," Cuatrel said. "But a funny thing happened. I was angry as hell, and then it was like one day I woke up, and I didn't miss 'em."

Pinkins said, "I know the feeling. I had the selfsame experience." He then guessed, "That's when you wrote the letter."

"I did, sir. Because I felt, in my heart, that you needed to know I had changed—thanks to you."

Pinkins said, "I appreciate the sentiment. But I just inherited the law and made sure it was followed."

"Well, thank you, sir. I uh…." Cuatrel put down his fork for a moment. "About those mannequins…I feel real bad about those. I took 'em all down."

"I appreciate that as well," Pinkins said.

"So do my neighbors, I reckon," Cuatrel said. He thought a moment, then said, "Well, most of 'em. There's some worse than me. You've never seen so many Confederate flags in one ten-block area. But, uh, still…I don't know what I was thinking. I'm sorry."

"You needn't apologize for exercising your First Amendment right," Pinkins said.

"Oh, but I do," Mr. Cuatrel said in his continuing contrition. "That was abusing those rights, sir. Crying fire in a theater and all. Disrespecting the Constitution. That's what that was. It just took me a while to realize is all."

"Democracy is complicated," Pinkins said.

Cuatrel said, "Not really. I'm just a thickheaded dumbass old vet with no class."

Pinkins felt bad for the older man. "Now, don't be too hard on yourself, Mr. Cuatrel. You're a decorated veteran.

And we are grateful for your service. As to the expression of your...ideas, you saw the light and realized the folly of your intent. So, no harm, no foul."

"Hell," Cuatrel said loudly. "I didn't know what my damn intent was!" He laughed. "I was just mad is all. Stupid. I blame it on the Busch Lite."

"Anger can make us do inappropriate things. Behave in... inappropriate ways." Pinkins fought hard to avoid using the word "stupid." He added, "Alcohol tends to make it worse."

Cuatrel nodded. "Tell me about it. Between the two, I ran off six wives."

"Six?" Pinkins said, either impressed or shocked. He had only been married once, to Daisy, and always figured that if she passed first, he would never marry again.

Cuatrel said, "That's why I got only that trailer left, and a 1983 Plymouth needs a valve job. If it weren't for Social Security, I'd be on the street." He thought of something and looked up. "Ya'll aren't planning to gut Social Security and Medicare, are you?"

"No, Mr. Cuatrel," Pinkins said. "That's the other party. We want to expand both. It was in our platform throughout the campaign, and I aim to honor those laws the same way I did GCA. I stated it unequivocally at the convention, and I intend to stand by it to my grave."

"I didn't watch none'a that crap," Cuatrel said. "Don't mean nothin' to me. It's why I don't vote."

"I see," Pinkins said, seeing himself inside his mind shaking his head outside.

"Anyway," Cuatrel said. "I'm awfully glad you accepted my offer to accept my apology in person. I mean, hell, I ain't nobody. Just a cranky old man with too much time on my hands is all. I'm amazed they invited me here at all." Before

Pinkins could comment on the raft of new information, Tommy Cuatrel said, "Aren't you gonna try that tuna? It'll knock your socks off. That's *my* campaign promise."

Pinkins said, "In a minute," though he had no plans to eat tuna salad from a Sizzler in this lifetime. He just sat, staring. Waiting.

Which spurred Cuatrel into action. "Oh. Yeah. The apology. Sorry. You probably have more serious matters to attend to."

"I do, Mr. Cuatrel," Pinkins said. "But right now, I'm here to listen to you."

Cuatrel stiffened his back to look official and dug in his shirt pocket, agents close by watching his every move as Roger Pinkins started to feel bad for the poor codger. He said, "You know, Mr. Cuatrel, you really don't have to do this. The letter was enough."

Cuatrel said, "Not for me. No, sir. I was wrong. Besides, wasn't much of a letter. One line is all. No eloquence to speak of. Nope, I was wrong, and it needs rightin'." Finding nothing in his pocket, he said, "Shit!" and stood up sharply, reaching for his back pocket. Agents were all over him before he was halfway to his feet, subduing him, locking him down, freezing any movement.

He did not appreciate the intrusion. "It's just my notes, goddammit, my speech! You already frisked me a dozen times. Damn near busted my hemorrhoidal polyps, fer Chrissake!" He held up his folded crib notes and waved them around defiantly. "See? Paper is all!"

As the agents assiduously followed protocol and began to release him *slowly*, Mr. Cuatrel opened the page allowing everyone to see that he had penned a short speech, Pinkins happy to see that the rest of their meeting would be over quickly.

As the agents stepped back, Carl Cuatrel huffed and sat down. He glanced across the table and said, "You don't care for tuna, do you?"

Pinkins said, "Not much. No."

Cuatrel barked at an agent, "Take that away. You shoulda known he don't like tuna and told me, for Chrissake. You beg me to come up here then work at makin' me look bad."

Pinkins registered confusion. "They…what — ?"

Carl interrupted to continue his indignant demand, "Now take it! Go on!"

He was yelling at Helga, who did not move.

No one moved.

So, President Pinkins said, politely, "If you wouldn't mind. The smell."

Helga nodded at the reticent waiter, who came over, lifted the plate with the scoop of foul-smelling canned fish, and took it away, being careful to deposit it deep in a bus bin, rattling it around as if making sure it would stay there at the bottom.

"Sorry," Cuatrel said. "As I mentioned previously, I rile easy."

"I understand, Mr. Cuatrel," Pinkins said, giving up hope on any clarification of how Cuatrel came to be here at this Sizzler at this point in time — at least from Cuatrel himself — and nodded at the crib notes. "Proceed, please."

"Thank you, sir," Cuatrel said. And he read, "Mr. President, it is with great humility and regret that I must say these words." He looked up to gauge the president's reactions, and precisely at 12:15 p.m. yelled, "NO!"

Carl "Tommy" Cuatrel then dove across the table, throwing his body onto the president's as a shot was fired.

Cuatrel looked shocked and rolled off the president onto the floor.

Pinkins said, "What—?"

Another shot was heard, and the president's head ejected blood and tissue onto the opposite side of the booth. As he drooped, a third shot was fired, and pieces of the president's brain pan were delivered onto Mr. Cuatrel's face.

Still alive but fading, Carl "Tommy" Cuatrel said, "Shit," again.

This time he really meant it.

The gaggle of agents had been caught off guard, taking precious seconds to assess from whence the shots came. One of their own provided an answer.

The unwilling waiter, himself a secret service agent with the highest clearance possible, as was required, said, "Life to America!" And shot himself in the head with the same gun.

As he fell dead to the floor, agents swarmed him, Pinkins, and Cuatrel, whose eyes were clouding. He said, "I just wanted to say I was sorry. Bastards tricked me…."

And he died.

CHAPTER TWENTY-FIVE

Down in the basement of the still "currently undergoing reconstruction" federal building in midtown, the string of explosions frightened Mike Cho and the two other Ball soldiers as now, several more rushed in wanting to know, "What's happening?"

Scattered gunfire was heard, then a crack team of combat-ready highly-trained Special Forces types flooded into the room, keeping a muzzle on everyone except David, who said, "Meet my backup, Mike. The men and women of the United States Marine Corps." He looked at Corporal Cho and said, "Semper Fi, *dude.*"

David Billows then reached back and tore the ridiculous shields off the wall, throwing them onto the floor with disgust. He told Cho and company, "Your little enterprise was over before it ever began. Enjoy Leavenworth. Maybe Gitmo. You're going to be there a while."

Cho objected. "But...the government can't use our military for police actions."

"Our?" David said. "So now it's '*our*'?"

"It's...illegal!" Cho spluttered.

"And what you clowns were doing *wasn't*?" David said.

"We were saving America!" Cho protested.

David said, "By killing democracy? Right. Always the same bullshit reasoning."

Cho said, with surprising eloquence, "Democracy wasn't working."

David Billows said, "No, I'd say it worked just fine."

***

Never-a-Sergeant Michael F. Cho and everyone else in the unused building were taken into custody and removed from Washington D.C. in unmarked prison buses, where they were taken to anonymous sites for military tribunals, convictions, and sentencing.

None would see the light of freedom shine on them again in their lifetimes.

Less than an hour later, Sally Hawkins was sworn in as president of the United States "in a secure location." Cal Worthing held a press briefing, Brian Williams reported on it—along with every other reporter on the planet—and the protests and counter-protests sputtered out as word spread on cellphones throughout the city, which became an instant place of mourning.

Some gun enthusiasts were, of course, delighted over Pinkins' death—and made fools of themselves on social media—but for the most part, America was shocked and disheartened. It had been a whirlwind three months. Now? No one knew what might happen next.

Someone knew—many someones.

***

In her first Oval Office address to the nation, President Sarah L. Hawkins decried the violent assassination of the last president of the United States, Roger John Pinkins, and declared a period of mourning. One week later, POTUS Hawkins gave her second address to the nation from the

Resolute desk. Meghan Carter and Jim Malloy reported it this way.

MEGHAN: "In a stunning announcement, a complete reversal of policy and federal law, newly sworn in President Sally Hawkins and Congress have come to an agreement to end the ban on guns in America."

MALLOY: "That's right, Meghan. The GCA is now officially history, folks. Gone as quickly as it came. I can't say many will miss it."

MEGHAN: "No, Jim, I doubt they will. As of noon tomorrow, gun manufacturing and sales will begin anew. Gun makers anticipate making close to a trillion dollars in sales in their first six months of operation since they were shut down nine weeks ago."

MALLOY: "It's a brave new world out there, once again. We now go to Belle South at the former home of Angelo Miller, the first casualty in America's war on guns."

The camera cut to the pile of ashes and rubble that had been Big Angie's house before he was shot, and his family opened fire, and they were shot. Belle South, the black reporter who had "won" the lottery to interview Angie Miller, strolled into frame looking more relaxed and confident than she had that fateful day.

She said into camera, "Meghan and Jim, this is where it all began, right here behind me, in what is left of Angelo Miller's once happy home here on Prairie Street in downtown Akron, Ohio."

***

In Colorado, Garreth Peters, the quietest one of David Billows' team at their compound, had put the lid back on the septic tank and recovered the drain field before David and Carlos made Kansas. When the two returned from their

Washington adventure, they were happy to find that everyone but Garreth, Marjorie, and the kids was gone, having fled when news of the president's murder and the secret plot to overthrow the government of the United States went public.

Details of the event—including video of the Schwan's truck with its hidden arsenal laid out alongside—rang too close to home, and everyone else ran for the hills—of Ecuador.

After the second night, David and Carlos hugged, and Carlos headed south to rejoin his family in Sedona. Though they felt good about what they had stopped, both hoped that their anti-subversive careers were over forever.

Garreth thought about staying, but another few days later decided to pursue a lost love in San Francisco—a set designer for a commercials house that had made a fortune creating ad campaigns for PetCo and Gravelly tractors. His name was Paul, and he was eager for Garreth to come out—to San Francisco—and give it another shot.

After David and Marjorie said the last goodbyes and were alone by the firepit by the creek in the late fading light of a warm and bug-free late-spring evening, she said, "So...."

David chuckled and held her tight, idly watching the kids night-fish for trout in the stream. He thought a moment and said, "I don't know."

"Will you ever?" she asked.

"I don't know that either," he said.

"You did what was needed," she said.

"I guess," he said.

"Didn't turn out the way you imagined?" she said.

"Never does," he said.

As they both stared into the robust column of flames, she said, "Which side do you think you were working for?"

After a moment of watching sparks rise into the darkening

sky, David Billows took a breath, let it go, and shook his head.

Glenn A. Bruce wrote the hit movie *Kickboxer*, and wrote for *Walker: Texas Ranger*, *Baywatch*, the original *G.L.O.W. Show*, and Cinemax's *Assaulted Nuts*. He holds an MFA from Lindenwood University and was an associate professor at Appalachian State University for over 12 years, where he taught Screenwriting, Acting for the Camera, and Video Production, which resulted in several awards for writing and directing. Glenn has had over 50 short stories, essays, and poems published in the U.S., Britain, Canada, Australia, and India. He currently judges a tri-annual short story contest, writes 1-2 screenplays per year, and recently finished his 17th novel.

www.ingramcontent.com/pod-product-compliance
Lightning Source LLC
Chambersburg PA
CBHW030329180626
46810CB00003B/1278